# JOIN UP

Editor: Hilary Smith
Front Cover Image: Martina Gates
Front Cover Design: Allie Gerlach
Back Cover, Spine and Interior Design: Daniel Choi
Proofreader: Gillian Campbell
Website: Lynn Jatania / Sweet Smart Design

ISBN: 978-0-9936837-7-0
Copyright 2015 by Tudor Robins

Visit Tudor at www.tudorrobins.ca

# JOIN UP

## TUDOR ROBINS

Island Series – Book Three

# Other Books by Tudor Robins

**Novels**
Objects in Mirror

**Island Series:**
Appaloosa Summer
Wednesday Riders

**Downhill Series:**
Fall Line

Every riding camp I attended taught me something, even if it wasn't always the thing I thought I wanted to learn when I first went there. This book is for those who have a special riding camp in their life, or memory.

# Chapter One

---

As my dad and I coast down the gravelled road, studded with the occasional massive clump of Canadian Shield granite, and overarched with reaching maples and oaks, and the imposing sign appears – Julianne Hills Riding Academy & Camp – my breath catches.

When Carly asked if I'd come work with her at her mom's friend's summer riding camp, I knew it was an expensive place. The fees posted on the camp website made university tuition seem like a bargain. But the site also promised a friendly, low-key atmosphere.

This huge sign is grand and formal – the very opposite of low-key.

When we get right up to it, though, and turn the corner onto the steep driveway, the peeling paint is clear.

The paddocks lining the drive are white-wood fenced, but when we pass the brick house, fronted with four white columns, they give way to unpainted split rails and, from what I can see, it seems like electrical fencing maintains order even further back, behind the stable yard.

My dad stops our hulking truck next to Carly's mom's little Miata and looks over at a tidy two-storey brick building. "That looks nice."

Carly's mom laughs. "It is, but that's not where our girls are staying."

"Oh?" my dad asks.

She's shaking her head. "No, that's the brand new dorm. For the big-paying students in the school year. The idea is that the campers should rough it. They'll sleep in the classrooms." She points to a row of once-white, now dingy, portables, linked together by an unpainted boardwalk running from front door to front door.

Sure enough, as we watch, an older man and younger guy are shoving a mattress through one of the narrow doors. The door slams shut in the younger guy's face and his curse rings clear in the late-morning quiet.

I'm already getting a feeling there are two camps here. The bright, shiny, top-of-the-line place fee-paying parents see, and the behind-the-scenes close-up I'm getting.

Camp-Good-From-Far-But-Far-From-Good.

I make a mental note to call it that in my first message to Meg.

I picture her reading it, laughing, telling Jared and a spear of uncertainty twangs at my gut.

I shake my head. *It'll be fine. It's a summer job. It'll help pay my university tuition. It's with horses. Carly's here.*

And, if worse comes to worst, I'm here for three, three-week sessions. That's it, that's all. Anyone can do anything for nine weeks. Right?

My dad taps my shoulder. "You hungry Lace?"

I smile at my dad. "Yeah. Come to think of it I am."

We're in a family restaurant in Julianne, which turns out to be an intersection of two highways marked by a flashing light strung high in the air with a random orientation that makes it unclear which drivers should stop, and which have right of way.

Maybe the idea is just for everyone to slow down.

At first, I'm glad our booth is huge – it must be meant for six people, at least – because Carly's mom has her brow furrowed, head tilted to the side, and is saying things to my dad like "I was so sorry to hear about you and Maddie. What a shock," and "I heard she's living in Kingston?"

If I was any closer to them I'm afraid my inner voice would become outer, asking, "How could it be a shock? When was the last time you actually saw my mom and dad together?" and "Yes, my mom's living in a waterfront mansion in Kingston with some construction guy who owns half the city and, yes, he's also half my dad's age ... or nearly, anyway."

But Carly's keeping me busy talking about how she kind of wishes she hadn't agreed to come be a counsellor at her mom's best friend's riding camp because, of course, when she said she would, she didn't know she'd get together with Cade.

When she says his name, she bats her eyelashes, and her cheeks pink up, and my stomach lurches.

*Cade.*

I close my eyes and smell the last of the apple blossoms, imagine sun on my face, remember the itchiness of the round bale pricking my back, and arms, and neck, and my pulse rushes as I relive Cade's lips on mine. Cade saying, "Oh my God, Lacey, when did you get so pretty?"

And it's true I've forgotten the exact way his mouth felt against mine, but his words are saved in my mind, along with that feeling – shocked and pleased – at being noticed, being chosen, being wanted.

Until he chose Carly.

She doesn't know. To her it wasn't a choice he made between us. To her there was nothing, and then there was Cade, liking her. And I guess it really is true what happened between Cade and me was nothing, because he didn't tell anyone – never let on in any way – not the way he does with Carly.

He was at the ferry dock when we left this morning, leaning her against the Miata, his hands in her back pockets, with her mom and me standing to the side, trying to pretend we didn't notice how far his tongue was shoved down her throat.

My love for my dad swelled when the truck horn sounded, sharp and sudden, and Cade jumped off Carly.

"I should go," I heard him tell her.

"I'll walk you to your truck," she said, and when they passed me, hand-in-hand, he touched his ball cap.

"Bye Lace. Have a good summer." Then his gaze dropped to my chest and he winked.

I hate him. Which sucks. What I really want is to feel nothing about him at all, but now, as Carly prepares to flick through her latest photo album of adorable Cade shots, my own cheeks are reddening. "I've got to go to the bathroom!" I flee the booth, passing the waitress carrying a tray laden with our food orders.

It looks delicious. I can't imagine eating any of it.

I should have eaten all my lunch and ordered a second meal, too.

The huge stainless steel bowl on our table contains a twisted white mass, with a light pinkish stain to it, studded by some unidentifiable lumps. I think it's supposed to be spaghetti.

I stare at it.

*Breathe, Lacey.*

The food has to get better.

*Right?*

I mean they can't charge the fees they charge here, and serve food like this.

*Can they?*

The regular cook mustn't start until tomorrow.

*Yeah, that's it.* This is how they feed the staff, and the culinary standards will pick up tomorrow.

OK. That sounds reasonable. I'm choosing to believe it.

I glance at Carly seated to my right, and catch her gazing at the bowl with her nose wrinkled and lips pursed.

I shoulder bump her. "For real?" I whisper.

She coughs. "Let's hope not."

The bowl was carried to the big round table eight of us are sitting around by a girl with a jaunty ponytail and the most beautiful skin I've ever seen.

The cups and the pitcher of watery-looking Kool-Aid were picked up by a freckle-faced girl with dark hair, called Miranda. Her mother also went to university with Carly's mom and the woman who owns this place. Jan. I still haven't met her.

The plates are here courtesy of me after one of the other girls at the table – her skin as acne-riddled as the first girl's is clear – looked up from her phone long enough to say, "The dinner bell went – aren't you going to pick anything up?"

I've never been to camp. Don't know how things are done, but I followed Miranda to a long counter at the front of the big dining hall where a lady wearing a hairnet handed me a stack of multi-coloured plates and eight napkin-wrapped knife-and-fork bundles.

I guess we're all supposed to eat out of this communal central bowl of cooling, tangled pasta. The thought turns my stomach.

I am *so* not a group person.

So, why did I come here?

There's a dinging of glass, like when I went to one of my

cousins' weddings and people wanted the bride and groom to kiss, and we all turn toward the next table over where a tall, thin woman has risen to her feet.

"Jan," Carly mutters under her breath.

*Aaah* ... my new boss.

I'm jealous of her hair. A weird thing to think about a woman at least as old as my dad. But, unlike my not-quite-curly, not-quite-straight, half-assed-wavy hair, hers is severely straight and wickedly shiny. The part, down the middle of her scalp, could have been guided by a ruler. Each side falls in an absolutely unbroken sheet to just above her shoulder.

I can't tell if her hair is blond or silver, but it doesn't really matter. It's bright and pretty.

Her voice is deep. "I would like to welcome you all to another summer at Julianne Hills. Those of you returning know the traditions and quality we uphold here."

Someone, somewhere at our table, kicks somebody else. I can't pinpoint the kicker or the kickee, but I know it happened.

Jan continues. "For those of you who are new, welcome, and I trust you'll soon love this place as much as the rest of us already do."

"Returning staff, please help new staff and, of course, Owen, Fitch and I are always here to help any of you."

The older, mattress-hefting man smiles. His eyes crinkle at the corners like my dad's.

The younger, door-slammed, swearing guy raises his eyebrows. He looks like nobody I grew up with. Nobody I went to school with.

From the careless-but-perfect loose curls in his dark hair, to concave line of his cheeks between his cheekbones and jawline, to his t-shirt that just skims and touches places on his shoulders and chest, without clinging, he looks like money, and good breeding, and athletic prowess, and arrogance.

We don't have those where I come from. We just see them on TV.

I'm waiting for the rest of Jan's speech – wanting to know the rules, and what's expected of us, and how things work around here – when she says, "Well, the campers arrive tomorrow, so enjoy dinner and get a good night's sleep," and she sits down.

Carly sighs. "Allow me." She picks up the tongs protruding from the bowl and frees a clump of pasta which she settles on my plate.

"So polite," I mutter.

She grins. "Anything for my hometown bestie."

"I never knew you cared so much."

She laughs, and reaches to serve Miranda, and I'm left staring at the now-much-colder mass of sticky spaghetti lumped on my plate, wishing I was home, on the island, grooming Salem, having a still-not-very-tasty-but-at-least-warm meal with my dad.

I'd even go back to the part-time job I thought I hated, waiting tables at the Grill, sometimes getting my butt pinched by drunk guys from Kingston who didn't know Danny, the owner, would take them outside later and shove them against the siding, and twist their collars tight around their neck, and breathe, "You don't ever, *ever*, touch her again. Get it?"

And if I was still there, and Carly was here, maybe in some weird set of circumstances, Cade would kiss me again, and tell me Carly was his second choice, and it was all a mistake, and I would be noticed, and wanted, and chosen again.

I think I'll never fall asleep with the bed springs poking my hips through the thin mattress.

I'm wrong.

Because I'm well and truly out – zonked, bonked, probably snoring – when the creaking, and swaying of the metal bunk hauls me out of sleep.

"Come on, Lace!" It's Carly.

Disorientation sweeps through me. Why am I with Carly in the dark, at night? "Wha'? Where? Huh?"

"You must be starving. I am. Miranda worked here last year. She's going to get us some food."

I'm so sleepy it's sucking – like quicksand – I visualize my body slung deep into the bunk, and can't imagine hoisting myself out.

But Carly's right – the hunger's right there, too. Like a vortex in the middle of my body. Empty. Spiralling. Needing to be filled. "I ... OK ... gimme a sec."

She backs away, which is good, because I less climb down, more fall.

The years of horseback riding have been good for something. I let my knees go soft and it doesn't hurt, although it's alarming how hollow the floor sounds under the thin layer of all-season carpeting covering it.

I put my hand out and steady myself against the wall. That's the good thing about sleeping in a converted janitor's closet stuffed with a bunk bed – it's not big enough to fall over in.

I giggle, and my muscles wake up enough to bear my weight, and I follow Carly to the rickety screen door on the room we'll be calling home for the summer.

⟨⟨⟩⟩

Goosebumps. Sharp gravel poking the soles of my feet through the thin rubber of my flip-flops. Wet streaks across my arms and cheeks from the dew already forming on the bushes we push through.

Then, "Shhh ... quiet." And we're slipping inside the dining hall building, but this time going in a back door, following Miranda.

"Don't let it ..." Miranda's back by my side as the screen door stutters to a close. She grabs it, eases it shut with a small click. "It rattles like hell otherwise," she whispers.

We cross a dim room full of big shapes and she stops in front of one very big shape, lifts a lid, and a light washes out.

"Voila!"

Oh. Wow. Ice cream.

Ice cream like I've only ever seen before in the refrigerated display cases at the general store. Massive cylindrical vats, full to the top.

"Cookies 'n Cream or Mint Chocolate Chip?" Miranda asks. She doesn't even offer the Tiger Tail and my respect for her grows. Tiger Tail is such a crap ice cream flavour.

I just stare, but Carly steps right up. "Cookies 'n Cream! Is there whipped cream or anything?"

Miranda's digging at the pristine surface, prying chunks loose and dumping them in Carly's bowl. She juts her chin over her shoulder. "Look in that cupboard."

"Won't they notice?" I ask. "Won't somebody notice?"

Miranda shrugs. "Yeah ... and?" She grins at me. "What're they going to do?"

"I ... uh ..." My tired mind gives in and I grin back at her. "I guess you're right. Mint Chocolate Chip, please."

Carly turns a can of whipped cream upside-down, froths it over all our bowls, and I dig in. The sweet softness of the cream, the sharp mint, and the bitter edge of the chocolate chips swirl together on my tongue. *Mmm ...*

"So, what's your story?" Miranda points her spoon at me, then at Carly.

Carly's mouth is full and I've just swallowed, so I answer.

"Um, well, we've known each other forever. Right Carl?"

She nods. "But then we really became friends when we did this musical ride together a few years ago."

I laugh. "I haven't thought about that in ages. We were good!"

Carly smiles at Miranda. "Then I decided horses were a little too mucky for me, and I stopped riding, but for some reason this horse-crazy girl decided to stay friends with me."

"Ha! That's her way of saying she went from horse-crazy to boy-crazy."

I instantly regret saying it. Carly turns her spoon upside-down in her mouth, and her eyes go dreamy as she stares off into the distance. She makes a pining, longing, "Hmm ..." kind of sound.

Before she can say Cade's name yet again, I jump in. "So, anyway, Carly knew I wanted to make money to go away to university, and she knew they needed a riding instructor here, so ..." I wave my spoon in the air like a magic wand, "... she made it happen, and I'm really grateful, even if I didn't expect to be sleeping in a room the size of a prison cell with her."

Carly's eyes snap back to me and she gives me a shoulder nudge. "Oh yeah? You'd better not snore ..."

Miranda breaks in. "Well, at least there's just two of you. I might have a huge cabin, but I'm going to have a dozen girls sleeping in it with me and you can guarantee more than one of them will snore ... or worse." She pauses. "Speaking of which, enjoy these last few camper-free hours, because tomorrow there will be little girls everywhere you turn."

We finish our ice cream standing up, in the washy greenish hue thrown by some safety light on some appliance or other, and my empty stomach fills, and I think, *This will be OK*. I like these girls, and I made it through the first day.

Or, technically, half-a-day, but who's counting?

◇✕◇

I've managed to figure out this much; that I have to be up by the crack of dawn.

Which is no surprise.

I mean my job title is "Riding Instructor." Ergo, horses. Ergo, early mornings. And, probably, late nights – but you know, one-day-at-a-time, one-hour-at-a-time. I'm not thinking about the night, yet.

I leave Carly deeply asleep, dark lashes lying across her smooth cheeks – a bit like an angel – while sawing out a rhythmic buzzing snore that woke me even before my alarm could – less angelic.

Karen, the barn manager, meets me at the gate just like she said she would.

I met her yesterday. She's small and kind of ... *bent*. I don't know how else to describe her – maybe gnarled? Like the twisted apple tree on our front lawn at home. Low enough to reach the apples right out of the branches, but so strong it's resisted decades of island winds that frequently gust over a hundred kilometres an hour.

"Morning," I say. As is the island way. Even when you have a stonking head cold. Even when you were up until two a.m. with a sick calf. Even when – as I've only been a couple of times, but man, it hurt – you're nauseatingly, head-poundingly hungover, it's always a good morning.

My dad won't start work until everyone's said it. He got more militant about it after my Uncle Rob died. It's like some sort of mantra. Some sort of safety spell to keep us all safe as we go about our daily duties.

Karen obviously doesn't know that, and she's my boss, not the other way around, so I have to content myself with the fact that she nods at me and hands me a lead shank.

We step into the long, dew-coated grass. Swirls of lingering mist, and cotton-candy-sticky spider webs part around our legs.

There are shapes on the horizon, and they're our target. Heads down, grazing, but they know we're coming. As we close in there's a shifting around the edges of the herd, ears flick, and a few heads lift; nostrils flare.

"C'm o-o-o-on!" Karen's voice sends my heart hammering up against my breastbone. Holy crap, that woman can project.

She calls it again; the long melodic word flowing seamlessly out of her compact body, filling the field.

Now they're all at attention. All ready to move.

Karen nods at me again – this time with direction. *Left* she says wordlessly. First day and I can already read her mind. It must be destiny. I veer left, trying not to laugh.

Several of the horses are already walking, heads low and in front of them, reaching, bobbing. These are the ones who know they're going to end up inside no matter what and, hey, there's hay in there, so why not go now and get there first?

Normally I like my horses with a bit of spirit, a bit of spunk, but in my newly minted role as riding instructor, I already respect these acquiescent leaders.

Karen and I are here for the rest of them. The resistant ones. The dawdlers or would-be rebels. The ones who hang back, or try to circle away. The ones who know no amount of hay is worth getting kicked in the ribs and yanked in the mouth all day. I get it, but it's called earning our keep. We all have to do it. Why else would I be here this summer?

I watch Karen on the other side of the field, and copy her. I get my lead shank swinging in a wide circle. I step out to get behind stragglers, urge them to join the main herd. I start with "Git!" and "Move along!" and, because it's fun, graduate to "Hyup!"

And they move. Not always happily, not always quickly, but they move. Eventually they're all jogging and there's a pleasing tattoo of hooves, making the ground sound almost hollow.

Karen's left the gate open and they stream through, and up the ramp to the barn and inside they all branch off into this aisle, or that. They slot themselves into a series of standing stalls.

When we get in, there are just a couple standing in the aisle, staring patiently at stalls they obviously think are theirs, but are already occupied. In one case Karen takes the waiting mare and guides her one stall over. "In here you stupid old thing." In the other case she backs the interloper out of the disputed stall. The waiting horse slips in, and she puts the first one in a nearby box stall. "You'd think he'd remember we moved him to a box stall, wouldn't you? But no – he keeps going back to that narrow old standing stall."

Then she brushes her hands together. "There, that's the herd in. You'd better get off to breakfast before you miss it."

⟨⟨⟩⟩

Breakfast might be what keeps me from starving to death here. That and the ice cream. I wonder what a nine-week diet of breakfast cereal and Mint Chocolate Chip will do to me?

My barn duties mean I've come in at the tail end of breakfast, with most of the girls I ate with last night already done their meals. They've scattered to different tables around the dining hall, propping up signs that read Cabin 1, Cabin 2, and so on.

This is how I figure out who's a counsellor – like responsible for a cabin full of kids – as opposed to those, like me, who are "staff." I'm one of four riding instructors, but the only one who lives here. Karen told me yesterday there are two other women who come in each day, and Jan teaches the most competitive kids. Carly is the arts and crafts leader. She's going to be in her element surrounded by glitter glue and ribbons all day – pretty much always having something cute, or pretty, or trendy for the campers to work on. She finishes eating about three minutes after I sit down – "I'm going to help Miranda decorate her cabin sign!" she says – and I'm left at an empty table.

Until Fitch sits down across from me.

He doesn't say hi. Doesn't look at me. He puts a magazine called "Swimming World" on the table beside him and starts flipping through as he spoons cereal into his mouth.

Swimming, huh? It explains a lot. The broad shoulders. The narrow hips. The general air of no-fat-and-a-lot-of-lean-muscle. It doesn't explain the long hair, though. Don't guys who swim keep their hair short? Maybe pretty-boy can't bear to let go of his pretty curls ...

"What?" His voice snaps me out of my wild internal speculation.

Instead of being polite, like I've been raised to be, and embarrassed, like I've been socialized to be, I'm bold and prickly. Maybe it's Karen, refusing me my 'Good morning.' Maybe it's the sheer excitement of having an edible meal in front of me. "What, *what*?" I counter.

"You're staring at me."

"You're reading a magazine."

"I have this very special ability. It's called peripheral vision. You might have it, too. Most evolved human beings do." He pauses, raises his eyebrows, and waits just long enough to let me know he's questioning the level of my evolution. "Anyway, it allowed me to see you staring at me."

*Ouch.* Is this how being bold and prickly always goes? It's nasty ... but kind of fun, too.

"You might have heard of this other big word," I say. "It's

called narcissism. It's having a blown-up view of your own importance, and a craving for admiration. It could make you think somebody was staring at you when they were just reading the clock on the wall over your shoulder." I point at the big clock, conveniently hung on the dining hall wall opposite me.

Then I decide to go.

Fast.

Before he can say something smart in response.

Because it's early, and I'm tired, and I'm not used to this witty insult thing. I'm not sure I can keep up.

I stand, lift my bowl and cup, and say, "Bye!" in the lightest, breeziest tone I can come up with. And as I walk away, just in case he's watching, I sway my hips a bit.

Which is probably narcissistic of me.

Unfortunately my peripheral vision isn't good enough to see if he's looking.

# Chapter Two

There's no riding scheduled for the first day, thank goodness, because the morning is manic, with horse trailers pulling in, one after another, unloading horses ranging from nice-quality and much-loved, to oh-my-god-do-not-get-a-scratch-on-this-one-because-you-can't-afford-even-his-left-ear. Fortunately those ones won't be my problem after today – they belong to Jan's students – but every time I'm there to take the lead of one of them as they unload from their very shiny trailers, I'm the model of horse-handling care and attention. Two hands on the lead shank, walk by their shoulder, nice wide turns into the barn, and into their big box stalls.

To the owners, dropping off their horses, I look like I know exactly what I'm doing.

When they're not looking, I'm constantly asking Karen, "Is that horse in the right stall?" "Where do I put his organic, fair trade sweetfeed?" "How should I attach the five stall toys they sent with him?"

Not for the first time, I think Jan's putting an awful lot of faith in the say-so of Carly's mother that I know what I'm doing.

⟨⊗⟩

Lunch is disgusting. I think it's supposed to be macaroni and cheese. Really, it's just more glumpy pasta. I've only been here twenty-four hours and a theme is emerging. What's wrong with sandwiches? Just plain old sandwiches. That you make yourself. That you can put things you actually like in.

While I'm not eating I gaze around at the filling tables. Most of the counsellors have at least half their campers sitting with them. The staff table is more full than at breakfast. There's a part-time tennis instructor who comes in each day. Why she'd actually choose to eat here, is beyond me.

Fitch doesn't show up. Which is a relief. I bet you anything he's having a nice peanut-butter-and-jam sandwich in his big brick house with the four white columns in front.

Carly takes most of my attention. To say she's worked up is an understatement. Carly just found out after breakfast this morning – along with the rest of us – that when campers are on site, there are no cell phones allowed.

Not even if you're the camper-daughter of one of the richest families in the province who brought her very own bubble-wrapped horse to camp with her.

Not even if you're a desperate staff member facing three times three weeks away from the newly discovered love-of-your-life.

"Cell phones are not part of the Julianne Hills philosophy," Jan said this morning, and handed bins around for us to surrender our phones into.

Carly ran to the back of the room, and was still thumbing urgently when the bin finally reached her.

With all our cell phones dutifully collected, Jan said. "Please don't try to get another phone and use it. If we see them, we'll confiscate them. You'll get these back when the campers leave at the end of the session, and you may keep them until the next group arrives. You can always communicate with your friends and family using the telephone there," – she points to a not-private-at-all cubby at the back of the dining hall – "Or using the computer, which has an internet connection, in the staff mailroom."

And then she went. I'm already getting used to Jan's sudden disappearances.

So, sans cell phone, Carly wants to talk to me more than ever. It's like my cousin was for the first few weeks he quit smoking. He'd find you anywhere – in the general store, on the ferry – and say, "Talk to me. Keep me company. Otherwise I'm afraid I'll have a cigarette."

I let Carly's words wash over me. "So unfair ..." and "... even legal?" and "This food sucks." Although I notice she's eating it and, when I push my plate in her direction she tucks into mine, too. If she lets food be her fill-in for her phone, Cade's going to have a shock when he sees her again.

Someone taps my shoulder, and Carly shuts up. Fast. I turn around to see Jan. "Riding orientation is at three o'clock in front of the tack room."

She doesn't explain what orientation is – I assume it's for the campers, but it sounds like somewhere that information gets disseminated. Which could be very useful for me. I nod. "OK. Thank you."

All the counsellors have the same time off – essentially when their campers are in other activities. Riding with me, playing tennis with the part-time instructor. Presumably swimming with Fitch. I have a weird dead zone right after lunch when the summer sun will be at its hottest and the horses will have a couple of hours to loaf in the shady barn.

My gamble that this might be a good time to login to the ancient desktop in the staff mailroom was right. The big box of electrical parts whirrs and clicks quite a bit, and is dog slow, but I login and sure enough Meg's name is bolded in my inbox.

I've been lots of things since I arrived here. Uncertain, overwhelmed, tired, and almost perpetually starving. Right now, though, seeing Meg's name, is the first time I've been well-and-truly homesick.

It hits me like a punch to the gut. For a minute the twist of pain is so tight I can't breathe or cry. Then I suck in oxygen, and that almost makes it worse, because it's as though it frees up all the rest of my body to work. My tear ducts to cry, and my throat to sob.

I just sit for a minute, and rock in the chair, with my arms crossed in front of my chest, and I blink at the screen through blurred eyes and wish I could stroll casually into Jared's barn or my Aunt Jane's kitchen. Wish Meg and I could saddle Jessie and Salem and hack them to the river. Wish I could argue with my brother, Will, and stick my finger down my throat when I walk into the family room and find him, limbs intertwined with his girlfriend – my former best friend – Bridget.

There's a noise – a click – at the screen door. I whip my head around. Oh crap. Just what I need. That'll make the next nine weeks better – to get labeled as a crybaby on the second day – before I even have to face any campers.

But nobody comes in. The door doesn't open, and I decide it was probably a barn cat. As with all stables, this place boasts an assortment of cats who may not possess both their eyes, or both their ears, but appear to have no trouble catching mice.

I shake my head. *Be realistic Lacey.* I'm not the only one working hard this summer; we all have responsibilities, and we all have to get on with them. My dad and Jared – and Will, too – are working every angle they can think to bring in money from the farm. And my mom leaving my dad – well, even though it didn't shock any of us, and the old platitude probably is right that it's the best thing for both of them – we still don't know what her lawyer's going to ask for in terms of the divorce settlement.

Meg's working in town – she has an apartment downtown so she can walk to her relatively high-paying job at the university every morning. "When my prof offered, I just couldn't turn it down, Lace. The money's really good ..." We both know Jared would kick and scream before accepting money from her, but we also both know farming income can be precarious. If she and Jared are going to have a future together it makes sense for her to want to pad her bank account.

And Salem. Well, there won't be any more rides on Salem. I've mostly come to accept it – the slip and trip at an event – not over a cross-country jump, but unloading from the trailer. It didn't look like much, but all the rest and rehab we've tried in the months since hasn't come to anything. I'm giving her this entire summer off, and part of me thinks maybe – maybe – when I go back she'll be well enough to ride again. But she's not as young as she used to be and ... well, if it works, great. If not, Salem has a paddock for life, so the story's not as bad as it could be for some other horse, but still ...

Even though I know I can't just run home and have everything be normal, it's still what I want.

I click Meg's message open.

Hey Lace,

Miss you already. I know, I know – I shouldn't say that because it'll make you miss us, but it's true, and I never want you to think it's easy for us to see you go.

You, Lacey Strickland, are brave, brave, brave to go off

and live somewhere else for the whole summer, when I know you hardly even like sleepovers on the island.

And you're also kick-ass to jump in and raise the money you need to go to university.

And I bet anything there's at least one amazing horse waiting for you there. And maybe a new great – if not best – friend. And I know it's a beautiful place. I'm definitely coming up to see you more than once this summer.

Things here are good. You know how crazy hyper Jess is these days when I ride her. I wish I could get over more … anyway, last night Salem ran up and down the fence line following us. Part of me thought I should try to stop her, to keep her leg rested, but then part of me thought if she was feeling good enough to run, then great.

I wondered "what would Lacey do?" and decided you'd let her run, so that's what I did.

Jared says hi. We're all going to have a big meal when you come back on your break at the end of the first session. Your Aunt Jane says you have to tell her what you want and she'll bake it for you, plus enough for you to take back.

Work is surprisingly good. I like it. And, you see, I didn't think I would, so the same thing will probably happen to you.

Let me know what it's like there!


Later,
Meg


I do, and don't, know what to say back. I want to let the words in my head tumble out of my mouth, the way they always can with Meg. I want to rehash the debates we've already had a dozen times. Like, will I ever find another horse I'll love riding as much as Salem? And, am I selfish for wanting to go away to university, even when I could study in Kingston, and commute from home, and save all that rent money?

I know Meg's answers, but I want to hear them again. *Yes,* I'll love riding another horse, but in a different way. *No,* I'm not selfish – my dad wants more than anything for me to go away to school and I'm taking the burden off him by earning my own tuition.

I even, almost – a little tiny bit – want to talk to her about Cade. It's the one thing I've never told her. About how, at the first pork roast just before spring turned to summer, he took me into the narrow sweet-smelling outdoor aisle created by the twin rows of round bales, and he backed me up until the hard wall of packed hay curved into my back, and how his kisses tasted like strawberry shortcake and beer, and how I waited all the next morning, and then the next day, and then the rest of the week, for him to call me and, instead, the next time I saw him he was holding Carly's hand.

I kept it as first a delicious secret – to be revealed when he was officially my boyfriend and we showed up as a couple at the next pork roast – and then as an embarrassing secret; one I was so glad I'd never mentioned to her, because how humiliating was it that I thought five minutes between the hay bales meant he wanted to be my boyfriend?

But now I'd do anything to talk to Meg, and I'd talk to her about just about anything.

Except not by email. I just don't type quickly enough to keep up with the flood of thoughts tumbling through my brain and, anyway, with this grindingly slow computer, there's no way I could get the message written and sent before the orientation session in the barn.

I send the lamest reply ever – a stupid happy face – and logoff so I can head to the tack room and hopefully find out what my job is for this summer.

# Chapter Three

A couple of the girls are taller than me. Several look older than me.

I feel like a massive poseur standing on this hay bale off to Jan's side, in front of them. Like I'm some kind of expert. Like I'm any kind of authority.

Of course, the ones that are my responsibility are most likely the smaller ones at the front. And they worry me for another reason. Many of them don't look big enough to be getting on horses. They're little wisps of things with sparkly unicorn tattoos on their forearms (I sense Carly's work), and gaps from missing teeth in their smiles.

I'm supposed to help these tiny creatures control the big, luggish, pushy, and very savvy school horses Karen and I herded in this morning?

Piece of cake ... *not*.

The barn rules Jan's laying out for everyone are standard. Nothing earth-shattering. But it's good for me to witness their delivery so I know all the riders should know them, and abide by them.

Once Jan's finished the common part of her discussion, she nods sharply, twice. "OK, then. Intermediate and Advanced riders, you'll come with me and we'll have a discussion about goals, and strategies to achieve them. Novices, you go with Lacey."

I've been nodding along with all the rules:

"Sweep up after yourself." *Nod.*

"Always clean your tack after riding." *Nod.*

"Don't hose your horse off inside the barn – that's what the outdoor wash stall is for." *Nod.*

"Novices, you go with Lacey." *Nod ...* oh, wait, *crap.* Go *where* with Lacey?

I clear my throat. "Uh ..." and realize I'm raising my hand, too. *OK, that's not authoritative Lace, lower the hand now.*

Jan turns to me – one eyebrow so far up it lifts one side of her shimmering bobbed hair. "Yes?"

At the exact same time a little girl says. "Are we going to do the grooming thing now?"

Grooming. Yes. That sounds good.

I stretch a smile across my face and tell Jan, "Nothing." Turn to the little girl. "Yes, we are. Do you want to pick a horse to get started with?"

Oh my goodness. They're hopeless.

What am I going to do with nearly twenty hopeless students? How am I going to have them riding in an end-of-session horseshow if they can't even groom?

Which lots of them can't.

Are there lead line classes? Even if there are, I can only lead one of them at a time. Besides, I'm pretty sure their parents haven't shelled out the equivalent of a semester's worth of my university residence fees to watch their kids be led in a pony-ride-circle after three weeks at camp.

I chew on the inside of my lip.

OK, some of them are fairly competent.

Like the little girl who asked if we were going to do the grooming thing.

She walked up and down the aisle, gave a little squeal when she found the horse she wanted, and quickly and confidently led him out of the stall and clicked him onto cross-ties.

There are a couple of others who also asked me if they could pull horses out and I nodded and said, "Uh-huh."

Stalling. That's what I was doing.

But it gives me an idea.

I clap my hands, twice, then three times fast. It's what my grade four teacher used to do to get our attention, and we all had to clap back. From the back of the aisle one lonely little clapback drifts to me. I laugh. I guess some teachers still use it.

"What's your name?" I ask the little girl who clapped.

"Amanda."

"OK everybody, if I clap like that, it's because I want your attention. If your hands are free, you can clap back to show you're listening. Otherwise, just listening will be fine!"

It was right after I asked Amanda's name that I realized I hadn't introduced myself, and Jan's introduction was non-existent, other than her perfunctory, 'Novices, you go with Lacey.'

I take a deep breath. "I'm Lacey, and I'll be your riding instructor for the next three weeks. I have an appaloosa mare at home ..."

"Oh! Appaloosas are my favourite!" calls a girl from the side.

"Great, yes, her name is Salem and she's very smart, and we've done lots of things together including eventing, although she can also go Western, and pole bend, and calf rope."

I pause. They're all staring at me. I seem to have barn cred. *Thank you Salem.*

"So, you won't all ride at once – this big group will be divided into three groups, and each group will ride twice a day at ..." I rack my brains for the schedule Jan rattled off in the last few minutes before she started speaking to the big group of riders, "... 8:45, 9:45, and 10:45 in the morning, and again after noon at 3:30, 4:30, and 7:00. Your counsellor will tell you which group you're in."

There's shifting, and murmuring, and I clap my hands again. This time at least half of them clap back. Progress already.

"You need to be here at least fifteen minutes before each ride, and you need to stay at least fifteen minutes after. Why?"

"Oh! Oh! Oh!" I point to the little girl who looks like she's literally going to jump out of her jodhpurs, and she takes a deep breath. "To look after our horses, and groom and tack up. Or untack."

"Exactly. Which brings us back to grooming. We need to make sure you all know how to do it so you can get yourselves ready tomorrow morning. Who's a grooming expert?"

Three bold hands shoot up.

"Good. Who's quite good at grooming?"

Four more hands rise, including Amanda's.

"Excellent. So, you and you, go with Amanda. And you and you go here ..." I divide them all up – the truly clueless with the at-least-semi-competent – then I wander around and watch the more experienced girls teach the others.

I only intervene when they give blatantly incorrect information. "Um, no, you should actually *not* use the curry comb on your horse's fetlocks," or, "No, even if you think there's nothing 'bad' in the sand ring footing, please still pick out your horse's hooves after you ride them."

For forty-five minutes I don't think about going home, or being kissed by Cade, or how bad dinner's likely to be. For three-quarters of an hour I feel capable of teaching these girls at least something – or at least of manoeuvering them to teach each other.

Now if I can just figure out how to get the better riders to teach the rank beginners ...

*One thing at a time, Lace.*

For now this is good.

⟨⟨⟩⟩

It's Miranda and me alone in front of the ice cream freezer tonight. Carly started out with us, then peeled off to try to get some uninterrupted internet time on the staff computer.

"How was your day?" I ask Miranda.

It's a throwaway question – one you ask because you're supposed to – but she pauses with a spoonful of ice cream halfway to her mouth, and a smile spreads across her face. "Great! I love camper arrival day."

"Really?"

She nods. "I adore kids. I want to be a teacher. This is the best job I can imagine."

*Oh,* is what I think, but in the face of her enthusiasm it makes me feel petty and pathetic. Instead I say, "That's awesome."

"How was your day?" she asks.

"It was ..." I hesitate. What was it? "It was better than I expected."

She nods. "It's intimidating at first." She lays a hand on my arm, cold from where it's been cupped around her ice cream bowl. "You'll do great. People like you."

27

I fight the urge to protest. Snort. Tell her she's crazy. "Thanks," I say.

I swirl some ice cream around and let it melt in my mouth. "That's a nice thing to say."

# Chapter Four

---

How does this ever work?

The bad news is it took more than half of today's riding session to get my first class mounted, with girths tight enough that they're not likely to end up under their horses' bellies, and stirrups somewhere in the knees-slightly-bent-but-not-tucked-up-under-the-armpits-region.

The good news is that more than half of today's first riding session is done.

I wonder what my class would look like from above – an aerial view – it could probably be used as some sort of scientific study of random movement. Six horse-and-rider combinations wandering in six unpredictable patterns and directions.

This won't do.

But I can't figure out how to fix it. I mean, they literally can't steer. Like not at all. I thought novice meant ... well, *novice* ... I thought it implied some level of basic knowledge with lots of room for improvement.

I had no idea it meant complete-and-total-rank-beginner. Like, without guidance would probably sit on the horse backward.

I'm tempted to just let the clock run out on this lesson but

I have to get them dismounted and out of this ring somehow and I can't see how I'm going to manage that without introducing at least some level of order.

I watch as a fat brown pony sticks his nose up the bum of a taller grey pony. Fortunately the extensive time I spent with each rider on their girth and stirrups means I now know all their names, and I'm about to say, "Sarah! Keep your pony's nose away from Rachel's pony!" when the penny drops and a very faint and distant memory washes into my consciousness.

A ride.

That's how beginners learn.

They go in a ride.

It takes me another five minutes to actually get them arranged into a ride. Six equines, standing nose-to-tail; they look like elephants in the circus. But they all have relaxed ears and none seem very perturbed by their close proximity to one-another.

Probably because – duh – they're used to going like this, and most instructors aren't dense enough to take half-an-hour to figure it out.

My lengthy observation of their wandering at least allowed me to identify one of the peppier horses, and I've put him at the front of the group.

I stand by his rider's side. "Now hold your reins properly, like I showed you. Yes, thumbs up. Good. And give him a nudge with your leg ... and another nudge." Nothing happens until I cluck and growl – then the horse's ears sweep back, and he steps forward right away, and I feel vindicated. I might have no idea what I'm doing, but I fooled a school horse – he thinks I'm a nasty riding instructor.

The final ten minutes is smooth as butter. I stand back a bit, and work my way down the line of riders, all walking because their horses are happy to keep up with the horse in front of them.

"Sarah! Thumbs up! Rachel, heels down! Ava, eyes ahead. Everybody – every single one of you – straight back!"

Oh, wow. Now this is easy. This is cake. I could do this all day.

Should I make them change rein across the diagonal? The question swims into my head, and I let it swim back out again.

*Don't rush things, Lace.*

After all, I have three weeks with these kids.

⟨XX⟩

Things that are making me believe I can do this:

- I taught all three of my lessons this morning, and nobody fell off.

- I walk past Miranda on my way to pick up my lunch, and she's laughing at something a camper's saying, and I remember, 'Best job I can imagine.'

- The hair-netted lady behind the lunch counter hands me an egg-salad sandwich. I can eat this!

- While I chew, and swallow, and enjoy every bite – and while Carly tells me word-for-word the content of Cade's latest email to her – my mind does mental math. I have over two thousand dollars saved from working at the Grill. The entrance scholarship I earned will cover my tuition. I'm two-and-a-half days into earning another three-thousand dollars. Which still isn't enough to get me through the whole year at university, but it'll definitely get me started.

- Small arms circle my shoulders, and the small hands that clasp in front of my neck nearly choke me, but the happy little girl voice saying, "Lacey! Lacey! The best riding instructor ever," melts my heart and I have my own, personal Mirandaish moment.

- I have two hours off now, when nobody else does. I've already figured out this will be my shower-and-check-email time. I have shampoo and a towel in the bag at my feet.

So, all in all I'm feeling accomplished, not starving, not-quite-broke, and anticipating being squeaky clean as my flip-flopped feet slap the smooth-worn dirt path between the big dining hall building and the smaller pool house.

This is where we're supposed to shower – all the staff and all the campers – there's a reason I'm coming when they're all busy.

Of course Fitch doesn't have to worry about overcrowded showers, or when he'll get to check his email. As far as I can tell, he saunters down to the pool at about 1:00 each afternoon, teaches swimming for a few hours and then goes back home where he probably sits in his air-conditioned house, and plays video games, and eats junk food.

I come to the end of the row of cedars lining the back of the pool enclosure, and start along the more open side, where nothing grows in front of the chain-link fence. I squint at Fitch. OK, maybe he doesn't eat junk food all day. I doubt his surf shorts would sling so low on his hips if he did.

And I guess he must do some serious swimming some-where bigger than this pool, to get those muscles across his shoulders and running along his arms.

Still, though, I can't imagine what it's like to work a few hours a day, and know where your university tuition's coming from – not just for one year, either – and be surrounded by this huge complex that your family owns.

Whatever. It would mean living here all the time, and while I'll make it through the summer, I already miss see-ing the St. Lawrence every single day. The rolling hills here are scenic, and make for some interesting cross-country approaches, but I miss the swaying hayfields stretching right to the shore. Miss the sky which, somehow, is just so much bigger, and bluer on the island.

I blink. It's Monday. And I get to go home for a visit two weeks from Saturday. *Oh, that's a long time ...*

I shake my head. One step at a time. One riding lesson at a time, one pilfered ice cream at a time, one shower at a time.

I reach my hand out to pull the pool house door open and Fitch yells. "Hey! Tick-Tock!"

*What the ...? Who the ...?* He is so weird. I yank the heavy door toward me.

"Tick-Tock! I'm talking to you!"

I turn and he's looking right at me.

"What?"

"Tick-Tock. You know; clock girl. I need your help. You work here, right?"

"Uh, yeah. Except for the next hour-and-a-half when I don't work. I'm about to have a shower."

He twines his fingers through the links of the fence. "I'm afraid not. We have a pool fouling."

"A what?" I don't even know exactly what he means but it sounds bad. Sounds disgusting, in fact. "What kind of pool fouling?"

"The worst kind."

"Well, I'm glad that's not my problem." Except, if I'm so sure it's not my problem, why am I not gone? In the building, behind a locked shower room door?

Fitch just does that eyebrow raising thing again.

"I hate ..." I almost say, 'I hate the way you always do that with your eyebrows,' but this time my manners kick in before the words come out. "... I hate how I never get any time to my-self here."

"I knew you'd figure out it was your problem."

"Don't push it. What do you need?"

Turns out what he needs is most of my time before I have to go back to the barn and teach.

"Do you want to fish out the poop, or figure out what to do with the kids?" He points first to a dark mass in the bottom of the pool, then to a half-a-dozen little girls lined up in their swimsuits along the pool deck.

"Where did ...?" I look at the poop, then at the girls.

He laughs. "Girls! Tick-Tock here thought one of you did this." The girls throw their hands in front of their faces and giggle and whoop. Ava, from my first riding lesson, points to the other side of the fence where an exiled Jack Russell terrier is sitting on his haunches, ears tipped toward the girls inside. "It was him!"

Fitch turns to me and drops his voice. "They smuggled him in with them – thought it was funny." He faces the girls again. "Now Julianne Hills girls, what do we bring to swimming lessons?"

They all dance on their tiptoes, hands raised in the air. "Bathing suit!" one yells. "Goggles!" calls another. "Towel!"

"Do we bring dogs?"

They all shake their heads at the same time. "No-o-o-o ..."

I watch him during this exchange. Maybe if I'd first met him here, poolside, joking with these campers, I'd think he was sweet, and funny, and – I don't know – more normal. Maybe I've been too hard on him ...

"So, girls, Tick-Tock here is going to take you somewhere now."

*Hold on.* "Uh ... no thanks. I'll do the poop."

I'm already being swarmed by little jumping-bean girl bodies. "Lacey! Lacey! Where are we going? Why does he call you Tick-Tock? Is he your boyfriend?"

That eyebrow goes up again. "I think they want to be with you."

I suck air in through my nostrils. Clench my fists. "You are such a ..."

"Such a what, Tick-Tock?"

"Don't call me that."

"You never introduced yourself to me, so I have no idea what to call you. Please enlighten me."

"Call her pretty!" says one girl. "Call her bee-yoo-ti-ful!" says another. "Call her tonight!" Ava dissolves into peals of laughter and doubles over. When she stands up again, she high-fives the girl next to her. "Did you hear that? 'Call her tonight?' I am so funny!"

"OK girls. Come on. Change room, let's go, go, go." I give my signature hand-clap and the girls who were in my riding group, clap back.

"Go!" I repeat, and shoo them into the pool house the way I shooed the herd in from the field this morning.

# Chapter Five

---

I'm almost too tired to rouse myself when Carly kicks the bottom of my mattress from her spot on the bunk below.

But, oh, I am hungry.

"OK, coming, coming ..."

This time, when we creep outside, easing the screen door shut behind us, and barefoot down the creaky wooden steps, it's not just Miranda waiting for us. Ponytail girl, from my dinner table the first night, is standing there, too.

When my eyes slide to her, Miranda whispers, "The other two are coming, too. They're just taking longer to sneak out of their cabins."

I know exactly who she means by "the other two." These girls have formed a tight threesome from day one. Their tables are close to each other in the dining hall, and whenever cabins gather, for any reason, they plunk their campers down together. I know the three of them go somewhere at night, but so far it hasn't been to have ice cream with us.

It's petty of me, but while we wait in the long slivers of light thrown by the nearly full moon, with the rhythmic chirping of the crickets and batting of fluttering moth wings around the porch lights ticking the seconds by, I hope they won't make a habit of joining us.

They finally come, with the one in front complaining, "Those little bitches in my cabin. I swear they sit up and watch me. God, it took forever before I could leave ..."

Miranda's shoulders twitch. "Bitches" won't have gone down well with her.

We fall into a single file line, quiet until a bat swoops through the pool of light thrown by the yard lamp near the dining hall. The girl in front of me ducks dramatically, "What the ...!"

"It's just a bat," I whisper.

"Just the most disgusting creature that ever lived," she hisses back.

*OK.* Note to self: just shut up.

As we back up in front of the kitchen door, waiting our turn to get in, I turn to Carly. "No computer tonight?"

She sticks her tongue out. "I went earlier. The door was locked." She shrugs, sighs. "So I guess I'll have to console myself with extra whipped cream."

Miranda's quiet and quick, scooping ice cream into bowls, handing them around. "We should go outside somewhere," she says. "There are too many of us to keep quiet in here. Plus we should probably sit where we can at least see your cabins." She juts her chin at one of our newly acquired threesome. "Your kids are pretty young."

The girl shrugs. "Sure. Whatevs. But I'm not bringing my bowl back when I'm done."

"I will," Miranda says quickly. "I'll bring them all back."

There's a big picnic table, half-obscured by a willow tree at the edge of the common green. Sitting at it we can watch the boardwalk running along the front of the cabins. On the bench next to me Miranda takes a deep breath once we're all settled there.

"Here." Ponytail-girl pulls a tiny bottle out of her pocket. "A little something extra for your ice cream."

"What is that?" Carly asks.

"Peach Schnapps."

"Mmm ... gimme," one of her friends says, holding her hand out for it.

The three of them splash the liqueur over their ice cream, then hold it out in our direction. While Carly hesitates, Miranda says, "Uh, no! I'm responsible for a bunch of twelve-year-olds."

When I shake my head, too, Carly follows suit. "Um, no thanks."

It's ponytail's turn to shrug and say, "Whatevs. More for us."

Carly turns to me. "I cannot believe Fitch pushed his kids off on you this afternoon."

Because, left with a dozen campers at loose ends, I'd decided to take them to Arts and Crafts where I figured there was always scope to weave an extra friendship bracelet, or make a shell pendant. And I was right, Carly was amazing. She hustled them in, and got them busy, while mouthing, 'What?' to me.

"Long story," I'd said. "They're supposed to be swimming with Fitch. But there was a pool – uh – *incident.*"

Ava giggled. "Yup. A dog pooped in the pool!"

I'd left the displaced campers with Carly and hurried back to the pool house to fit in the briefest of brief showers – more like a splash, really – before heading back to the barn to get my afternoon riders to walk on the opposite rein from this morning.

Carly licks whipped cream off her spoon. "Mind you, if I didn't have Cade, I'd be tempted to do just about anything for Fitch. He is so, soooo cute!"

Ponytail tosses her hair. "Oh, do not even think about it."

"Why?" Carly's eyes are wide and round in the moonlight. "Is he your boyfriend? I'm sorry, I didn't know ..."

Ponytail cuts her off. "As *if*. He's a lowdown, dirty skank. He usually picks a counsellor every summer and tells her lots of lies until she thinks he really likes her, then he dumps her." She pauses to scoop up a spoonful of Peach-Schnapps-laced dessert. "He might look good from far, but he's far from good."

I try to hold my smile in, but she notices my twitching mouth. "What?"

"Oh. I guess I was just wondering why he'd do that? I mean what's the point of making some girl think he likes her, just to walk away?"

She raises her eyebrows at me and I find I like the way Fitch does it better. It makes me feel less like a speck of dirt when he does it. "Well, sweetie, the thing is he doesn't just *walk away*. He gets what he wants first." She ratchets her eyebrows up another notch. "Do I have to explain what I mean, or do you get it?"

*Bitch.*

Miranda intervenes. "Who knows what that was supposed to be at dinner tonight?"

And since nobody can resist complaining about dining hall food, the tension diffuses in a chorus of, "Were those lumps pasta, or rice?" "No, I think they were just lumps in the sauce; you know, like from flour that didn't dissolve. My mom's gravy's like that sometimes." "Was there meat in there?"

I shoulder-bump Miranda. *Thanks*, I telepathize.

She shoulder-bumps me back. *You're welcome.*

# Chapter Six

---

Day Two of riding. Progress.

They start the lesson lined up on the centre line. They walk on the rail in one direction. They change reins across the diagonal. They walk the other direction. They line up again.

I'm amazed how low my standards have sunk because I'm elated that every single rider accomplishes this.

In each lesson, there's five minutes at the end, once they're all lined up, when I really, really don't want to disturb the peace, so I chose the best rider in every group and send her out on the rail for a solo trot.

"Watch her rhythm!" I tell the others. "See how she rises when his outside front leg goes forward? See how it's *one-two, one-two*, or *up-down, up-down*? Say it with me!"

I don't let them stop until every single one of them is chanting "up-down!"

Then I call the demo rider in, and sweep my arms wide. "That's your homework. To think about that rhythm. Once you feel it, the trot will be a piece of cake." I tap my temple. "It's mind over matter. Now go untack."

◇◇◇

And so, at lunch my mind lingers for a few minutes on my amazing instructing breakthrough, then starts racing ahead. Oh, the things I can do with my students now that they can steer their horses! We can ride circles, instead of going large the entire lesson. I can set up an obstacle course. We can go on a hack!

Oh, wow, a hack. Now that's a carrot worth dangling in front of them. Keep trying hard, keep paying attention, and we'll head out, across the big cross-country field, and take the path with the beckoning opening right beside the stone wall, the one that disappears into the woods growing up the side of the biggest hill around here ... the one I haven't even explored yet.

I should get on that. Should get on a horse.

"You just can't stop staring at that clock, huh, Tick-Tock? What's the matter? Important meeting to get to?"

I jump, then turn to Fitch. "This time I was staring into space, actually. As in savouring the peace and quiet. Relishing my solitude. Enjoying being alone." I throw in an experimental eyebrow lift at the end of my speech. Two can play at that game.

He unloads his food off his orange cafeteria tray, bends to put the tray under his seat, then straightens, looking right at me. "Listen. About yesterday afternoon ..."

"Uh-huh?" This should be good. But I'm not going to let it take long. Because this afternoon, I am definitely having a normal length shower *and* checking my email. Definitely.

While I wait for him to tell me what he wants to say about yesterday afternoon, he furrows his brow – it's a very expressive part of his face – and looks away. *What now?*

Somebody taps my shoulder.

Jan.

I take a quick glance at Fitch. He's face down, a soup-eating machine. Not meeting his mom's eyes.

"Lacey?"

Of course I knew Jan knew my name – she used it in the third person when handing the novice / hopeless riders over to me – but it's weird to hear her use it to actually address me.

"Yes?"

"There's a pony that needs riding. He's a real ..." she hesitates. Her nose wrinkles in a way that makes it clear she's not going to say 'angel.' Instead she chooses "... handful."

"He's a boarder – owned by one of the intermediate riders – and let's just say, he's not an intermediate ride. I'll need you to pop on him and teach him some manners."

"Um ..." When I thought I needed to get on a horse soon, this wasn't exactly what I had in mind. "I see. When?"

She looks at her watch, then looks at my plate. "Well, it seems you still have your lunch to eat, so as soon as you're done will be fine. Just head over to the barn and tell Karen you're riding Shimmer. She'll show you where he is."

And she's gone. Leaving me staring at the food that's only still on my plate because I can't handle the thought of eating it, then staring at her son, who robbed me of my free time yesterday, while his mother's done the same today.

"You!" I say.

He turns away from his soup to face me. "Yes, you," I say. "This time I *am* staring at you because this is the second day in a row that I'm not getting a proper shower, or the chance to even check my email and see if anyone from home still remembers me, or to even just have two minutes to myself."

"And you're blaming me?" he asks.

I want to be so angry at him, but his simple question robs me of quite a bit of my pent-up fury. I hesitate. "Well ... for yesterday I do."

He blinks. "Fair enough. I guess I can't argue with that." I'm thawing a bit. I nearly like him, when he taps the watch on his wrist. "And you can't argue with my mom, Tick-Tock. Or at least I wouldn't recommend trying it. So you'd better pass me that food if you're not going to eat it, and get yourself over to the barn."

*What a ...* I can't believe I almost thought he was OK for two short seconds.

"You are ...!" I can't even think of words strong enough.

He's already got half my rock-hard lunch roll stuffed in his mouth. "Not hungry anymore, that's for sure. Thanks for the food; now off you go!"

Brat. Jerk. Twerp. Donkey.

Except he's not a donkey – he's gorgeous. A large pony, with a slight build, and a ridiculously shiny deep gold palomino coat. His mane and tail are creamy white, and four white stockings stretch up his fine legs. He's stunning to look at. And stunningly bad to work with.

He tried to bite me. Tried to yank his hoof out of my grasp while I was picking it out.

But the thing about this horse is he's got no staying power.

The bite didn't land, so he didn't try another.

I pushed him off-balance and held onto the hoof, and he sighed and gave up.

Now, with me on his back, he puts up a token protest in response to everything I ask him.

Me: Walk forward.

Him: No, it's too hard, I'd rather drag my feet.

Me: I said, walk forward.

Him: Oh, OK. If I have to.

At which point he moves into a flowing, lovely, energetic walk.

Me: Move off my left.

Him: No, I'd rather just go through the corners square, like this.

Me: This leg. Here. Move off it.

Him. Sigh ... fine.

And then he's flexed, and listening, and responsive.

Our biggest disagreement comes when Jan shows up and asks me to put him over a small four-stride line. He does the first jump beautifully, easily, then throws in a sudden deke to the outside.

I suspect this is the real reason I've been asked to ride him. I'm guessing he's been running out all over the place for his rider.

"Oh, no you don't." I sit down hard, form a barrier with my outside leg and hand, look ahead, over the jump and growl at him, "Get over it!"

He does. It's a messy, angled, stag-jump from a near standstill, but he's over the small jump, and he didn't get to run out and, hopefully he's got the message that doing what I tell him to is easier than breaking the rules.

"Take him around again!" Jan calls.

I do and, although I've got all my defences ready, I don't need them. He sweeps through the combination in four beautiful strides, stays dead centre over both jumps and never hesitates, even when we do the line the other direction. Even when Jan comes in and adds a third jump.

"OK, that's good. Walk him out."

He wasn't running out because of physical limitations. He's hardly broken a sweat, and he's breathing easily.

"He had his rider off twice this morning," Jan says.

I nod. "I'm not surprised. He's quick. Those run-outs can really throw you off balance."

"Not you," she says.

I shrug. "I was ready. He's the type to try anything once."

She shades her eyes against the strong afternoon sun. "So, what do you think?"

I kick my feet out of the stirrups and slide off his back. Run the stirrups up, loosen the girth. "I think he's very capable. I don't think any of this was hard for him. I think it's a mental game with this pony. He knows when he can get away with things, and he figures out pretty quickly when it's not even worth trying."

I start walking him in a circle around her. "That's why I'm not sure me riding him is going to do much good. I mean, sure, he'll go for me, because he knows I'll make his life miserable if he doesn't. But, unless she changes her riding, the minute his rider gets back on him, he knows he can get away with all that again ... and he won't hesitate to do it."

Jan sighs. "You're right. He doesn't really need to learn anything. The problem is he knows too much already." She meets my eyes directly. "This is the worst kind of problem for me, because now I have to either work some kind of miracle with his rider, or I have to somehow break it to her parents that they've essentially bought her too nice a pony, and she'd be better off with something a little less flashy and a little more reliable. Which, since they just shipped him in from Connecticut, I don't think they want to hear."

I give her a half-smile. "Sorry."

She waves her hand. "No, you're right. Short of getting you to warm him up every time she wants to ride him ..." She must see the look of horror on my face, because she actually laughs a bit – a short, sharp bark that takes me completely by surprise – "... which, don't worry, I'm not going to make you do, well, she's just going to have to learn to ride him."

I reach up, pull his ear toward me. "You're a little devil, aren't you?"

Not that he looks like one now. He looks like a ray of sunshine walking beside me. He looks like any little girl's dream pony.

"OK," Jan says. "You'd better get him put away before you have to teach again." She heads for the gate.

The bitterness rises in me again. No recognition that all my free time for today is gone. No thanks for that.

It makes me bold enough to ask this woman I hardly know – who's much colder and reserved than the people I'm used to dealing with – "Excuse me?"

She turns, eyebrows up. It must run in the family. "Yes?"

"How did you know I could ride him? I mean, you've never seen me ride. I was surprised, actually, you gave me this job as a riding instructor without any screening. What if I was terrible?"

The bark-laugh comes again – even sharper this time. "You may think I'm old and stuffy, Lacey, but I do know how to use YouTube. I knew you could ride well before you got here. Now, go. And untack quickly. Karen keeps cold drinks in a fridge in her office off the tack room. I'll tell her to give you a Coke once you're done."

My mouth waters at the thought of a cold Coke. I feel so cheap – to have been bought by the promise of a refrigerated soft drink – but I have to admit, I'm excited.

"OK, thank you." But I'm already talking to Jan's back.

It's only later, as I'm sitting in front of the desktop fan in Karen's office, sipping my cold drink, that I have time to wonder, what did Jan see on YouTube?

I shake my head. With the speed of the internet connection in the staff lounge, I'll probably have to wait until I go home for my first break to find out.

# Chapter Seven

By the end of the week all my students have trotted, on both reins. Now that this ride thing has floated back to me, teaching is quite simple. The first rider in line trots, with me correcting, and cajoling, and trying my best to find something to praise, then she peters out into a walk when she hits the back of the line, and I tell the next girl to trot on.

I want to take them on a hack on Sunday. I think they're ready to walk through the countryside. Slowly. And with grass reins on all of them.

They've been surprisingly patient – I was afraid I'd get all kinds of grief about "when are we going to go faster?" and "when can we jump?" but they all genuinely seem to delight in just having a horse or pony to ride and love, and in getting better.

They're good kids, and I want to reward them.

And at lunch, when Sarah, Rachel, and Ava sidle up to me and twine their skinny little-girl arms around my waist, and neck, and shoulders, and say "You look so pretty today, Lacey!" and "Thank you for our lesson Lacey!" and Ava whispers, "I got a care package and my mom sent something for you," and drops a brown paper bag in my lap, I want to reward them even more.

"Can I open it now?" I ask Ava.

She nods so hard I'm afraid she'll get a headache.

I open the mouth of the paper bag and look in. I gasp and look up at Ava, standing by my side, shifting from foot to foot. "Is this what I think it is?"

She nods even harder. My teeth would be rattling by now. "Sponge toffee. My mom makes it herself. And she dips it in chocolate."

I draw a piece out. "I can see that. Beautiful! Almost too pretty to eat ..."

Ava shakes her head. "Oh no, you have to eat it."

"Are you sure? Do you have enough for yourself?"

"Oh, yes. I already gave some to Sarah and Rachel and I still have lots. And she'll send me more."

"Well, I'll tell you a secret."

"What?"

"This is one of my favourite treats."

Carly's been watching this unfold and I hold a piece out to her. "Carly?"

She holds up one hand, and flattens the other against her stomach. "No way! I'm seeing Cade in a week. I have to look good." She collects her dishes together and stands to carry them away. "Thanks, though! You girls are sweet!"

I make a face at Ava, and Sarah, and Rachel. "Never don't eat something you want because of a guy."

Then turn to find Fitch staring at me. "What? You disagree? Trust me – there's no guy worth impressing enough to turn down sponge toffee. Especially Ava's mom's homemade sponge toffee." I sigh, and hold the piece I offered to Carly out to him. "Here. Never let it be said I don't share the love."

And then I take my first bite and it is sweet, salty, crunchy heaven, melting in my mouth and Fitch takes a bite, too, and I think maybe they should hand this stuff out in high-stakes negotiation rooms all over the world, because he doesn't say one single nasty thing to me. Just mumbles, "Mmm ..." and takes another bite.

⟨⟨⟨⟩⟩⟩

I know, in theory, campers are allowed to go on hacks, but I've got no idea of the protocol. I'm assuming I can't just take half-a-dozen brand new riders out on my own. I don't even know which horse I can use to lead the hack.

There's only one way I know to find out. Instead of heading straight to the pool house shower, I follow the leafy driveway to the great big brick house.

I cannot imagine walking up between those towering white columns and ringing the doorbell of the very heavy looking front door. This is the country. This house must have a friend-lier entrance. I walk around until I come to a side porch with just a screen door, letting what afternoon breeze there is blow through it.

I make no effort to be quiet on the steps leading up to the door. I'm hoping somebody will hear me, and come to see what I'm doing, and I can ask them to find Jan for me.

No such luck.

I'm standing in front of the screen, with no doorbell in sight, and nothing obvious to knock on, feeling like quite an idiot.

At home – on the island – I'd just walk in, calling, "Hello! Yoo-hoo! It's Lacey!"

But I'm not on the island anymore.

I decide on a partial island approach. No walking in, but I clear my throat and lift my voice. "Excuse me? Hello? I'm at the side door!"

After a while – after I've rapped my knuckles in a way that was quite painful, but made very little sound, on the door frame, after I've shifted from one foot to the other, and stepped down one step and back up again – when I'm just about to give up and leave, the dog decides to notice me. And all hell breaks loose.

It's the pool-fouling Jack Russell again, and he seems to want to make up for lost barking time, by turning himself inside-out making noise.

His small, barrel body tenses and his front legs come off the ground every time he yaps at me.

I lean forward, press my forehead against the screen and whisper, "Too little, too late – the jewels would be gone by now, buddy."

"What?"

My eyes fly up to see Fitch standing in the inner doorway to the house. "Oh, uh, nothing ..."

"Lacey?" Never before has seeing Jan put me at ease, but I'm so happy when she says. "Go on Fitch. I doubt she's come to see you. You need to be getting to the pool, anyway."

"Yes, you're right," I say. "I mean, I came to see you, not Fitch. I mean ..."

Jan pulls the door open. "Step in. Tell me what it is."

I accept her invitation and, inside the house, notice nothing at all. It literally doesn't smell like anything. No air freshener. No fresh baking. Weirdest of all, no horse smells. A house on a horse farm, owned by a horsey family, and their informal side entrance doesn't smell like manure, dust, peat, or barn. So, odd ...

Then again, *are* they a horsey family? Now that I think about it, Jan's the only one I've ever seen at the barn, and never on a horse. Does Fitch ride? I wonder ...

"Lacey?"

"What? Oh, yes. Why I'm here ..." I take a deep breath, think of Ava, and Sarah, and Rachel's happy little faces – of making them happier, "I was hoping to take my students on a hack on the weekend. Only walking, of course. And with grass reins. If the weather's OK ... but I'm not sure what I need to do. Would one of the other instructors come with me? Or one of your advanced students, maybe?"

Jan's not nodding, but she's not frowning either. While I wait, she takes a deep breath and says, "Yes, of course. A hack is something they look forward to. I'm glad you feel they're progressing enough to go. On the weekend, you said?"

I nod. "Sunday, I thought."

"Fitch can help you."

"Fitch? But ... swimming?"

She shakes her head. "There are no lessons on Sunday. It's the day the girls get to go into town to spend their tuck money. I thought Fitch might drive the van this year, but Owen can do it, like he normally does." She brings her hands together in front of her, like she's praying. "Yes, so you may hack your students in the morning, and Fitch will be your back-up rider, and then, of course, there is no second ride on Sunday."

"OK, well, thank you." I'm still trying to picture Fitch on a horse. I can't. Maybe that's because in my mind he's always wearing surf shorts and a lifeguarding tee. I reach for the door handle.

"Before you go, Lacey ..."

I turn back to Jan. "Yes?"

"There's a horse."

*Um, yeah, last I checked there were nearly a hundred of them.* "Yes?"

"He was left here by a camper last year. She brought him green broke only – too inexperienced a horse for her – much worse than Shimmer and his rider. She was terrified of him; wouldn't get on. When we couldn't get her riding him by the end of her session, her father refused to pay the second installment of her camp fees, and left the horse behind."

"Oh?" It's a strange story. I can't imagine just leaving a horse.

"I thought you might like to ride him."

"Me?"

"You're more than capable, you know, Lacey. You shouldn't doubt yourself."

I've never had a boss before, other than people I've known my whole life – my dad, Meg, Dan at the Grill – so I'm not sure how you say to a boss, 'I don't doubt myself, but I do doubt that you understand that if you averaged my pay for the summer out over the hours I'm working, it would be peanuts, and yesterday you took away my only free time, and now you're suggesting I give up the rest of my free time – which would turn the peanuts into crushed peanuts – and who, exactly, is going to profit from me schooling this green-broke horse you've had sitting in a field, because I don't think it's going to be me.'

I don't know how to say that without being fired, and I need this job (*you need this job, Lace, you need the money*) so I bite my tongue, and while I'm biting it she says, "Just ask Karen to show you the brown Ronson gelding, and see what you think. You can let me know."

"Mmm-hmm," I say. "Will do." And, again, I'm talking to air, because she's gone.

I walk back around the house, thinking *what now*? Am I supposed to drop everything and run and ask Karen to show me this horse now? Is that the idea?

No. No way. I'm having my shower, and I'm checking my email – assuming I can get to the computer, and it has a decent connection – and I'll see the horse later. When I'm at the barn. When I'm on duty.

Glad I made that decision. "So there!" I mutter under my breath, and somebody taps me between the shoulder blades, and my heart skips a couple of beats as I whirl around to face

Fitch. "What ...?"

"Here." He's thrusting something at me.

"What is this?"

"What does it look like?"

"An iPad."

"Very good. She can tell time and she recognizes technology."

"But ... what ...?"

"You've missed checking your email two days in row, right?"

"I ... yeah ..." I nod.

"And it's because of me, and my mom, so here. My iPad. It's logged in to the WiFi from the house. If you sit on that log over there, you'll still get the signal."

"But ..."

"Take your time. I should have been at the pool ten minutes ago. Bye!" And he's off, running. The muscles in his long, tanned, calves tensing and relaxing with each step. His too-long-for-swimming curls rising and falling.

I stare at the iPad in my hands.

I've been offered two gift horses in the space of five minutes. One I'm not sure I want. The second one ... well ... I head straight for the log Fitch pointed out and swipe the tablet screen to life.

I know when to grab an opportunity.

I should go. I still need to have a shower. I shouldn't push my luck with using Fitch's iPad.

But.

Jan said she knew I could ride long before I got here. How? I have to know.

With Fitch's super-quick connection, I surf to YouTube in no time, then do the simplest thing I can think of – enter my name in the search bar.

And, to my complete surprise, there's a hit. A clip of me, riding Salem, at one of our last events before her injury – the Sun Ray Horse Trials. There's actually a long list of horse-rider combinations running down the side of the page. Apparently somebody at Sun Ray videoed portions of everybody's round, and uploaded them.

Who knew?

I double-click my clip and suck in my breath as Salem appears, ears forward, popping out of a wooded part of the course. We sweep across, in front of the person filming, and the sideways view is of an eager horse, moving easily, with a beautiful cadenced stride. Of me, moving as little as possible, other than giving her a quick rub on the withers.

We pop over one jump – a standard log pile – and it's a beautiful fence. Easy, flowing, economical. No effort wasted in the air. No break in Salem's rhythm. She lands and picks up where she took off. *Nice.*

Then ... it all comes flooding back to me ... I remember now. Because the next jump isn't so normal. In fact, there's nothing standard about it. It's built around two trees, made to look like the masts of a ship. The obstacle is very broad, to the point where you could wonder if you were supposed to jump onto it, then back off again.

As we approach, you can see Salem's ears sweeping to me, then back to the jump. You can see her back off slightly.

In response, I sit deeper and her ears go forward again, to the jump, and she re-establishes her rhythm. Until ...

... *the dog.*

I remember.

The video shows it pretty much as it looked to me at the time. A dog, appearing out of nowhere – running across our path – very close in front of our path, and hesitation sweeping Salem's body.

I still remember how it felt – all her forward momentum backpedaling – her motion coming back under me and me thinking *Oh hell, as if the ship wasn't enough …*

It was absolutely decision time. We had to commit or bail – not just to stay on course – but to avoid getting hurt.

Half-a-dozen thoughts flashed through my mind in a split second. *The dog's gone now. Salem's fit. I'm fit. She can do this in her sleep. I trust her. We're good.*

"Let's go!" The audio isn't clear, but there's a definite exclamation there, and I know what it was and, as though I simply reached down and shifted her into a new gear, Salem picks up, too.

She responds – maybe to my voice, or my leg, or my seat – but more likely to my attitude.

She finds a faster, forward rhythm, and we approach the scariest obstacle on the course as though it's a cavaletti, and she flies it, and the last thing you see is her pretty little hind hooves in the air, and her rump galloping away.

It's exhilarating and upsetting in equal measures.

Well, now I know why Jan thought I could ride.

What she didn't know, was how much credit for that amazing recovery – that fantastic jump – should go straight to Salem.

My little mare. What a gem.

My little mare. Will I ever ride her like that again?

*I have to go.*

Remembering that time's passing is what keeps me from dwelling. Keeps me from crying.

Gotta go. Gotta shower. Gotta meet a new horse.

Life doesn't stand still for anyone. Not me. Not Salem.

# Chapter Eight

---

I come out of the shower room skin flushed – another benefit of showering mid-day; lots of hot water – and towel wrapped like a turban on top of my head. My clothes sit lightly on my scrubbed skin.

I'm humming, eyes down, adjusting my watch strap, when I run into something hard. "Whoa! Sorry!"

It's Fitch, and right behind him are the girls streaming in to change after their just-finished swim lesson.

"Thanks Fitch!" they chime. "Hi Lacey!" A couple of giggles rise from the throng. "Hi Lacey-and-Fitch!"

They flow around us, and disappear behind the change room door, and we're alone again.

I dig in my bag and pull the iPad out of the pocket I carefully slotted it into. Hold it toward him. "Thank you so much. It was awesome to be able to have a decent connection. It was really ... nice ... of you to lend it to me."

"Anytime." He reaches for the tablet and his hand brushes mine. My breath catches. *Cade.* That's what this reminds me of, kissing Cade.

I give a little laugh as I let go of the iPad. "Sure."

He stops. Rests his hand on my arm – this time deliberately.

I am so not used to guys I'm not related to touching me. He needs to stop so I can settle my breathing. "I mean it," he says. "You can use the iPad anytime. Just ask. I know ..."

"You know what?"

"I know it can be hard being away from everything you're used to." His eyes wander to the door I would walk out of to cross the common and get to the lounge where the staff computer is. The lounge where I sat and sniffed the other day, and thought I heard someone outside the door. *No ...*

The first two girls emerge from the change room, wearing t-shirts and shorts, chatting about what they're going to make in arts and crafts.

*Just look him in the eyes. Just say thank you.* "OK," I say. "Thanks."

"You're going to ask, right?" he says.

"Maybe."

"Promise."

I have to get to the barn. "OK, I promise."

"Ha!" he laughs. "Good. I'm sure you're not the type to break a promise."

On the surface he's being the epitome of thoughtfulness and generosity, but deep down I can't help but feel he's laughing at me – enjoying forcing me to do what he wants.

Whatever; if letting Fitch feel like he has one up on me involves me getting to check my email whenever I need to, I guess I can live with it.

"You're early," Karen says when I place my water bottle on the corner of her desk.

"Yeah, well, Jan said she wanted me to look at this horse. She said to tell you the brown Ronson gelding, and you'd show me where he is."

"She wants you to *look* at him?" The lift Karen puts on "look" tells me how well she knows her boss.

"Mmm ... she wants me to ride him."

"Let me guess ... in all your spare time?"

I shrug. "I guess so. I didn't say I would. I thought I should look at him first."

"Well." She looks at her watch. "No rush. Here ..." She opens the mini-fridge, pulls out two cold soft drink cans. "Sit for a few minutes then I'll show you this horse."

〈❁〉

*Uh-oh.*

He looks at me; dark liquid eyes peeking through a wavy, spilling, possibly-never-been-pulled forelock. His nostrils, surrounded by lighter, singed-looking tan hair contrasting with his otherwise dark-brown coat flare, and his flanks rise and fall as he inhales my scent.

My stomach flips, then flops, in a familiar way. I might not be used to the feelings teenage boys give me, but horses – there's no mistaking it – I just fell in love.

"He's cute, huh?" Karen asks.

"Just a little bit."

"Sweet, too," she says. "Goodness knows he hasn't been handled enough. He just mostly hangs out here with these old guys." She's already explained to me that the swaybacked, grey-flecked, slow-moving occupants of this field are all retired school horses, living out their lives, enjoying an all-you-can-eat grass-filled old age.

She reaches a calloused hand out to smooth his neck. "But he's good as gold. Mostly. Doesn't bite, or kick. No handling vices that I know of. Now riding ... that's a different story."

She pauses, winks at me. "Which, from the look on your face, you're going to find out for yourself."

I sigh. "He *is* adorable."

As we head back to the barn, leaving the gelding head up, ears pricked, staring after us, Karen says. "Why don't you ride him after lessons tonight?"

"The barn's supposed to be closed after the last lesson," I say.

"Uh-huh, and who do you think decides when the barn closes?"

◊◊◊

◊◊◊

en I come in from teaching the evening lesson, Karen juts her chin toward a box stall near the tack room. "I brought him in for you."

"That's so nice of you!"

"Just wait until all the kids are gone, and you can use the arena."

I wander over to the half door and peer in. The shadows are so deep in the stall, and the gelding's coat is so dark – barring the light bits around his eyes and muzzle – that it's hard to see him, until he steps forward to press his muzzle into my cupped hands.

"What's his name, Karen?"

She's working her way along the aisle, checking water buckets. "Doesn't have one ..."

I step back so I can face her as she walks back up toward me. "What? How can he not have a name?"

"Oh, I'm sure he does – probably in those legal documents the boss made his owners sign to say she was taking him to account for their unpaid fees – but he sure doesn't have a stable name." She shrugs. "He's just never used. Nobody has cause to call him anything, so ..."

*That is so sad.* I mean, I didn't like the thought of him just being turned out with a bunch of geriatric equines to laze his days away – what a waste – but not even having a name? Having nobody love him enough to even say, "Hey Buddy," or "Hi Lucky," or "Come on Billy," – well that's really upsetting.

I don't say it out loud, though, because it's not Karen's fault. She has enough horses to take care of – she has *more* than enough horses to take care of – I can see why this one, as long as he was healthy and fed, wasn't a big concern for her, but now I love him even more, just because he's been so *un*loved.

I turn back to the stall where he's retreated to the shadows again; just a flash of eye giving away his presence.

"Night," I say.

"What?" Karen's passing me now, on her way to check buckets in the next aisle.

"His name. It could be 'Night.' He's so dark. And it's simple." I shrug. "I don't know; I like it."

Karen nods, once, firmly. "Fine with me. Easy to spell. One syllable. No other 'Nights' in the barn. It's all yours." She pauses. "Or, it's all his, I guess."

She walks away, calling, "Bye, Night!" over her shoulder.

I've decided not to ride him.

Karen walks in as I pull the halter off Night's head and leave him naked in the middle of the arena. He's about Salem's size – I'm guessing about 15.2 – but he looks small in the big, empty space.

He's standing square on all four feet, head up.

His ears swivel. *This is new.*

His tail twitches. *I'm not sure.*

"What are you doing?" Karen asks.

"Join up," I say.

"Hmmm ..."

I don't know what her *hmm* ... means. Don't know if she thinks joining up is horse-whispering hogwash. Don't know if she loves the idea.

I just know I have to do what feels right, and with a horse that's been mostly left in a field for nearly a year – not even loved enough to be called by any name at all – and who, apparently was rather high-strung under saddle to start with, it doesn't feel right to just jump on his back.

Respect. I need to show it. Trust. I need to earn it. A bond. I need to build it.

At least I think I do.

Before I can second-guess myself, before I can turn to Karen and ask 'What do you think?' I take a deep breath and say, "Move along. Out on the track, Night. Let's go."

He shifts his weight away from, then back to me. He's just met me, but I'm already his rock in this new place. I'm not a horse, but I'm living and breathing, so he wants me to be his herd right now.

"Nuh-uh, you gotta go. Stretch those legs. This whole space is yours."

It's a big space too – there are no round pens here – the fully enclosed indoor arena is the next best thing. I hope it works.

I pick up the lunge whip, and when he sees it, Night moves off, head swaying with each long striding step as he walks, then quickens to a trot, then soon breaks into a canter, then a long series of bucks, and soon he's cavorting around the arena, twisting his neck, kicking up his heels, snorting and farting, and I can feel the smile stretching my face as I watch him play.

He settles down eventually, to a steady, cadenced trot and I think, *Step One.*

Except ten minutes later, we're still on Step One. Night's hooves are wearing a track into the perimeter of the rarely

used arena. Trotting, trotting, trotting.

I've got lots of experience lunging, so I'm pretty good at not getting dizzy, but this is testing my limits. I move into the gelding's line of sight so he'll at least change direction.

Which he does; right on cue. He dips his head and turns it to the boards while he skitters his hind end around and jumps straight back into the trot on the opposite rein.

This is when Night's lack of conditioning – of any work at all – starts to show. He's widened his nostrils, and in the light washing through the canvas arena roof, darker patches are becoming visible on his brown neck.

"This is taking a while!" I sing-song my voice; Karen's still watching but I don't meet her eyes while I say it. My focus stays on Night, but somehow stating the obvious helps.

"You're good." Karen's reply is quiet, but definite, supportive. It reassures me. Reminds me of all the things I've learned over the years of working alongside Meg. Where horses are concerned, we're never in a rush. Each horse has his or her own timeline. It'll take the time it takes.

The hunch drops out of my shoulders and I exhale. "OK."

I swear Night exhales too.

His head lowers, trotting slows, and his inside ear flicks to me.

I fight the urge to inhale, gasp, tense up, hope. Just keep him going. "Git up!"

I want to see it again.

I do. A few more steps, and that ear flicks in and his mouth starts working; licking and chewing.

*Ready.*

"Ready ..." Karen says it barely louder than a breath.

I've done join-up a few times. Sometimes it's easy, like it is when Salem and I do it. Sometimes it's a longer process, like now with Night.

No matter how it's going, this is always the toughest moment. The moment when I open my heart to the horse. When I think, *OK, come and get me,* and try not to let *please* show in the set of my shoulders, even if – for just a second or two – it's the only desperate thought in my mind.

I set the lunge whip down, take several steps away from it, and turn my back to Night.

*Please.*

I'm staring at Karen. She gives a tiny nod.

I wait and the whole back of my body tingles. Where is he? Why isn't he here yet? What if he doesn't come?

Karen mouths, 'He's watching you.'

*Oh, come on sweet boy. I want you, and you want me. You know it's true. We need each other. I want to pat you, and you want to be patted. Let's just get it over with.*

The words trip through my brain. The thoughts bounce around. But I stay completely still.

Karen's eyes widen, and smile, and ten seconds later hot breath whiffles down my neck.

I turn to face him. Turn to touch him. "Oh buddy." I make a fuss of him. Rub his smooth, hot neck, run my hand down his legs. "What a boy."

Then I walk away.

This is the moment when my heart always soars. Something about that no-big-deal way the horse moves off with me. Neck low and relaxed, head nodding. And how he stops when I do, and the look on his face says, 'You want to stop? OK, I'm stopping with you.' No rush. We're never in a rush.

And I step forward again, and he does, too.

We're a team. We're a pair. We're joined.

My heart always lifts during join up, but this time tears rise, too. For just a minute the unconditional love and trust this horse is giving me flood me with longing for those I unconditionally love and have left behind. I wish Salem was here.

Meg. Jared. I want to see my dad. I even – kind of, sort of – miss my brother.

But they're not here, and at least now I have something I didn't have when I woke up this morning. I have a partner. I have Night.

I blink the tears back, hoping not to let Karen seen them. She slides the barn door open for us, and as we walk by she says, "Nice."

When I'm counting my blessings here at camp, I guess I should count Karen, too. She might not say that much, but I like what she does say.

# Chapter Nine

Rain blows in and out all day Saturday. We struggle through morning lessons with damp ponies, and damp riders. It's cold, too, so everybody's shivering, including me.

After the last morning lesson, with the skies still hanging low and grey I tell Karen, "That's it – I'm making the call – we'll do horsemanship this afternoon. No riding."

Her eyes widen.

No afternoon rides means the stalls of the eighteen horses I use every day can be cleaned early, and they won't be as dirty to start with. It means Karen can kick off work that tiny bit earlier today. But that's only *if* we can get my lesson horses out. Normally the whole herd runs out together at the end of the day. Turning just mine out will need to be done by hand.

I look up and down the aisle at the six girls just finishing their grooming. I've been working with them for nearly a week. They're good kids. They listen. Except for maybe one, who's a bit of a daydreamer. I decide I'll walk behind her.

"Girls!" I call.

Six heads with helmet-flattened hair turn to me.

"How would you all like to turn your horses out before lunch?"

"Yes!" I hear, and another "Yes!" before "Lacey? Aren't we going to ride this afternoon?"

"We're going to braid this afternoon. Fun, pretty braids. We'll leave Ellie in," I point to a sweet mare with a long, sweeping mane – perfect for running braids – and tell her rider, "Jane, you can put her in her stall, and lead Button out instead."

Karen hurries ahead of us and holds the gate open for the six horses the girls lead out, plus the seventh I bring.

They go in neat, orderly, file. Karen supervises while each of them turns her mount around to face the barn before unsnapping the lead. There are no bites or kicks. No squeals or runaways. "Amazing job you guys. Want to bring out one more each for us, then you can run to lunch?"

At lunch I overhear one of my riders telling another girl in her cabin, "*I* turned my own horse out today." Her chest is puffed forward and she sits straight in her seat.

At the beginning of the week I was worried about doing enough with them. About getting them to canter, and jump, and be show ready. I'm slowly realizing how important doing less can be. Making sure they experience the simple pleasures of taking care of their horses. Of just being with them.

For a second I feel sorry for my current groups. They've had an instructor blindly feeling her way through teaching them. I shake my head. I still have more time with them. I can still try to do better. And next session – well next session I'll be a hundred per cent better.

It's the first time I've thought ahead to coming back here after my between-session overnight break at home with anything but dread, and now *I* feel proud.

Until Fitch sinks into the seat beside me. "Wow, somebody looks happy with herself."

*Don't slouch Lacey. Don't stop smiling. Don't turn red ... don't turn red ... don't turn ... oh crap.* Might as well tell Carly not to talk about Cade, or Miranda to stop ice-cream-eating raids – my cheeks are going to do what my cheeks are going to do, and that's burn bright red.

I turn to him. "I was happy ... until you sat down ... now I'm just irritated."

I sweep my lunch dishes onto a tray and walk away, without another word.

"So, I guess you don't want my iPad today?"

*Don't look back Lacey.* I cross my right hand over my left shoulder, give a dismissive wave and keep walking. *Not if it was the last iPad on earth.*

Forty-five minutes later, click-click, and re-clicking on the frozen staff desktop, I would do just about anything for that iPad.

Cutting off my nose to spite my face.

I do it. I know I do it. It's been my personal trademark ever since grade one when Hannah Beaumont handed out birthday party invitations to every girl in class – except me – and when her mother called our house to explain it was her fault, and my invitation was on the kitchen table at their house, and would I come, not just for the party, but for a sleepover as well, I'd refused to go. Told my dad, "No way. If she didn't want me at first, I don't want to go." I think I can even remember planting my hands on my hips.

And then on Monday I'd had to listen to all the girls talking about the indoor roller skating track they'd gone to, with prizes handed out every time the music stopped, and pizza and chocolate cake for dinner, and I'd stared out the classroom window and pretended I didn't care.

Meg's warned me about it too ... many times. "You cannot hold grudges against horses, Lace. Salem's already forgotten that stupid argument you two had yesterday. Her gift to you is a clean slate. Your challenge is to figure out how to go forward with it and avoid getting into the same battle again."

If I'd just kept my cool with Fitch – just let his comment ride and given him the benefit of the doubt – or even if I'd turned around at the last minute and said, "Your iPad? Now you're talking ..." I'd be reading about what Meg and Jared are doing this weekend, getting an update on Salem, finding out who's picking me up at the end of the session for the drive home.

Instead I'm staring at a sign-in page that isn't signing me in.

I sigh. Lean forward and click the whole computer off, count to five, then turn it on again for the next lucky victim.

Re-boot.

I have to see Fitch every day. He's my back-up for the hack tomorrow. I guess I should re-boot things with him, too.

Except, even though I drag my feet as I walk the beside the pool enclosure fence, Fitch doesn't look at me. Well, once, only. I half-raise my hand to wave, when I realize his eyes aren't on me, but at a camper on the deck in front of me, poised to dive in off the side of the pool.

"No Nora! Dives only off the board, and only when I'm watching!"

I sigh. It was stupid to think I could make up with him now, anyway. It's not like I could stop everything and talk to him in the middle of a riding lesson. Even if he wanted to talk to me – which, maybe he doesn't – he can't just come over to the fence and chat away.

I push into the pool house for my shower. I take my time. I check my watch. Try to figure out when his lessons will be switching. End up in the hallway outside the change room just as one group of girls rushes in, and wait to see if Fitch will be behind them.

He's not.

He's not, and he knows I'm in here. He saw me walk in, and he hasn't seen me walk out. This is where he found me yesterday when I returned his iPad. If he wanted to talk to me, he'd be here now.

So, he doesn't want to talk to me. Fine, I don't want to talk to him either. I shoulder my bag and head out the back door.

I'm busy anyway. I need to go see Carly and pilfer some Arts and Crafts supplies to make our afternoon braiding session extra sparkly and ribbony and fun.

And I need to see if I can track Jan down at the barn before lessons start and tell her I'll ride Night – maybe tell her I've named him Night first – because as much as it's going to be one more thing to juggle, there's no way I can walk away from that horse now.

I'm in love, so I'll make it work.

# Chapter Ten

———————

I eat dinner fast. Well, it's not hard to eat fast on grey meat nights. I eat the semi-limp green beans that come with the grey meat, and the reasonably soft roll from the side of the plate, and I tell Carly I have wicked cramps, and have to go to the bathroom, and that's how I get out of the dining hall with half-an-hour to spare before I have to take my evening group through their braiding exercise.

The exchange with Fitch has been gnawing at me all afternoon.

*Cut-off-nose-to-spite-face. Cut-off-nose-to-spite-face.*

It's all I can think about. Fitch was really, really nice to me yesterday. Kind of the way Miranda's been so nice to me about the ice cream. And I would never be so rude to Miranda.

I should apologize. I will apologize.

Fitch never shows up at the dining hall for dinner. Why would he? So I figure I can probably catch him at home about now.

I walk up the drive to the big house with my stomach churning.

Skirt around the side like I did before, rehearsing my story.

I never did catch up with Jan this afternoon, so if she answers the door I'll say I've come to tell her I've decided to ride Night. Then, hopefully, I'll somehow get a chance to talk to Fitch. To just slide in a quick "sorry." Make things right.

If Fitch answers, it'll be even easier.

I stand on the top step, take a deep breath in, reach my fist up to knock on the door frame, and voices carry through the screen door.

"You *what*?" That's Fitch.

Jan's voice. Even, calm, never raised, never ruffled, answers. "You can easily do it, Fitch. There are no swimming lessons tomorrow. It's in our best interests to make the campers happy, and a hack will do that, but Lacey can't take them out on her own."

"I don't want to do it."

"Fitch. It's a few hours. Riding. In the sunshine. Not exactly torture."

"Not from where you sit. It's the last thing I want to do tomorrow."

I drop my hand. Swallow hard.

Well, that's embarrassing. His mom's right – most people would kill to ride a horse through the countryside. There's only one reason I can think of Fitch not wanting to and that's ...

Footsteps. I realize they're coming this way. Oh crap. I really, really don't want to be seen now. I take a sideways jump off the steps; land on bent knees in the grass and press myself against the side of the porch.

As I retreat, crouching low until I hit the safety of the bushes by the drive, my mind circles back to the reason Fitch wouldn't want to join the hack tomorrow ... *me*.

# Chapter Eleven

This morning's warm-but-not-too-hot sunshine couldn't be more different from yesterday's scattered showers and cool wind gusts.

"Hack!" the girls were saying at breakfast. I heard it as I wove through tables going to pick up my morning cereal. Heard it in line waiting for watered-down orange juice to be poured. Heard one of my beginners telling one of Jan's advanced riders, "We're going on a hack today," and the experienced rider answering, "Lu-uh-cky!"

Between the promise of our hack, and the prospect of being driven into the village in the afternoon to stage a major attack on the candy bins in the general store, the girls are bopping, and buzzing, and humming as they groom their horses.

Much as I want to get on Night, that'll have to wait until later this afternoon. I need a dead quiet, dead reliable mount to lead my groups this morning. Something like the sturdy Clyde-quarter horse gelding I have saddled in the aisle for me, with his sister tacked up behind him waiting for Fitch.

*Fitch.* If he even shows up. He's not here yet, and now that I know how he feels about this outing, I'm already wondering if I can bribe Karen to ride with me.

I don't know if Karen even rides. Don't know ...

"Hey, Tick-Tock, to what do I owe the honour?"

"Huh?"

Fitch walks right up to the bay mare, slides his hand along her shiny neck. "I might ride more often if I got my horse tacked up for me." He turns to me, and that eyebrow goes up. "I assume she *is* tacked up for me?"

I cough. "Of course. Yes. I mean, I figured you were too much of a pretty boy to lift a hoof, or a saddle yourself so I did the hard work."

Three little girls are already swarming Fitch, jumping up and down around him like a litter of puppies. "Fitch! Are you riding with us? Are you and Lacey riding together? Are ..."

I give my clap, and they all freeze, turn to me and clap back. "Girls? Who is looking after your horses while you're over here?"

"Oh! Sorry Lacey!" They scatter off, but not before I hear one of them chanting, "Fitch and Lacey sitting in a tree, K-I-S-S-I-N-G ..." I press the back of my hand against my hot cheek. Hearing stuff like that isn't going to make Fitch like me any more.

He's whistling, though. Checking his stirrups. Adjusting his girth. "Did you leave it this loose on purpose, Tick-Tock?"

I snap my fingers. "Here I was hoping you'd end up under her belly."

He laughs. "I'll let you off the hook. I happen to know this one can blow up like crazy." He tugs at the mare's ear. "I've got your number, missy." She lowers her face and presses it to his chest. Small children and animals like Fitch. He's never prickly to them, the way he is to me.

"You ready?" he asks.

I nod. "If you are."

He lifts his voice and it carries the length of the aisle. "Let's get this show on the road so we can finish up and go buy some

Gobstoppers and Sour Keys ... who's with me?"

There's a chorus of cheers from our first group of riders, and our ride starts with sunshine, and blue skies, floating white clouds, and smiling girls.

I keep waiting for a horse to bolt. Or to pull a rider off over his head while he reaches for a particularly tasty patch of grass. Or to refuse to splash through the puddles left across the trail by yesterday's rain. But none of that happens. It's a charmed ride.

In fact, Fitch and I lead three charmed rides in a row.

"Wanna switch it up? You lead?" I ask him after the first group's hack.

He shrugs. "Sure, sounds good."

From my spot at the tail of the ride I catch glimpses of him – he's a natural rider; easy and relaxed in the saddle, while still being tall and straight. His long legs – the first time I've seen him wearing jeans – land just below the mare's girth. His hands are soft on the reins. Somehow, he even rocks his riding helmet – something not that many guys manage.

Not that I'm looking. I'm just glad his horse looks happy, he looks happy, my riders all seem happy. A happy morning. *Nice.*

When the last girl scampers off to lunch, I'm still untacking my horse. He's not exciting, doesn't double-thump my heart like Night does, but he's sweet, and he was just what I needed today.

I scratch his ear and palm him a carrot. "Good boy, Declan."

Fitch already has his mare put away. "Thanks for untacking her," I say.

"My horse. My job."

If I was looking to be swept off my feet, a guy with that attitude just might do it.

"You going to get lunch now?" Fitch asks.

"Uh, I still have to help Karen with turn out." No horses get
ridden this afternoon. It's a rest time for all of them. The herd
is quick to turn out, but there are a few boarders that need to
be hand-led into individual paddocks. "And then I'll probably
give her a hand sweeping the barn ..."

He cut me off. "You going into the village?"

I shrug. "Yeah. I guess I was going to." I grin. "I thought I
might stockpile some non-perishable food."

He wrinkles his nose. "The dining hall meals *are* pretty tox-
ic."

I wrinkle mine back. "Well, it's your family's camp – I didn't
want to say anything."

"That's unlike you Tick-Tock. You're normally pretty liberal
with the insults." Right away I think of yesterday. Of my may-
be-too-pointed insult. Maybe this is the time to apologize?

He continues, though, "Listen. Don't worry about lunch.
And don't get on the van for the village. Just meet me in the
driveway at the house in ..." He looks at his watch. "Forty-five
minutes."

"Why?"

But he's already walking away. "Less talking, more turn-
ing-out and sweeping, Tick-Tock." He taps his watch. "For-
ty-four minutes, now ..."

I close my eyes. The water's so hot it stings my skin – the only
way I feel truly clean. My conditioner-smeared hair is soft under my fingers. Grime, dirt, sweat, have all run off me, swirling
down the drain. Much as I love procrastinating in this steamy

shower, Karen shooing me out of the barn only bought me so much time. I figure I've got about six minutes before I'm supposed to be at Fitch's driveway.

One minute to scrub myself dry.

Another to smooth lotion on the sun-dried skin of my face and legs.

A minute to pull my clothes on – only sticking slightly on my still-tacky skin.

Thanks to the conditioner it only takes about thirty seconds to pull a wide-toothed comb through my hair, and I only need a few seconds to smear balm across my lips.

Which leaves two minutes to shove my stuff into my bag and sprint out the door.

I break from my run right before I round the bend that takes me into sight of the big house. *Breathe-breathe-breathe. Don't let him know you were rushing.*

I don't even make it into the drive before a Jeep backs out, turning sharply, and stops in front of me. "Hey, Tick-Tock! I was about to go off-roading looking for you. Get in."

There are no windows, that I can see, which is weird. I sling my bag in the back, and open the tiny door panel to let myself in. Fitch is talking the whole time. "Girls. They take forever. All 'I need to fix my hair,' and 'Wait, I need some lipstick.'"

I'm about to protest, when he narrows his eyes at me. "Then again, you don't exactly look like you bothered with any of that."

And what can I say to that? Because while I don't want to be labeled as a primping girly-girl, I'm pretty sure he just completely insulted me.

Fortunately he drives off, and first the rattling and pinging of gravel on the Jeep body then, as we pick up speed on the main road, the rush of air through the windowless windows makes it impossible to talk. I decide to enjoy my reprieve from the endless back-and-forth of verbally sparring with Fitch and pull my feet up under me, lean back, and let the buffeting blast of air be my makeshift hair dryer.

We start to slow when Julianne's single blinking light comes into view.

We pass under it, and roll past the general store with a big white van saying Julianne Hills Riding Academy & Camp on the side parked in front of it, and knots of girls sitting on benches out in front.

I'm self-conscious to be in a vehicle with Fitch, but the girls are too busy peering into each other's paper bags, and chit-chatting to even look up when we drive by.

"Where are we ..." The left-hand turn signal click-clacks me to silence.

Off the main road, into a narrow lane hemmed by buildings on either side and rutted with rain-filled potholes; we jounce and bounce and splash until we emerge into an informal parking lot in back where Fitch skews the Jeep at an angle into what I guess is a parking spot, then jumps out and walks to the back door of the closest building.

He hasn't looked back yet, and when he yanks the door open, taps his foot while I scramble to catch up. "Wait, wait, wait – it's all I've done today – you're lucky I like you, Tick-Tock."

"This is you *liking* me?" I duck under his arm and scoot inside ahead of him, and wish I hadn't because I'm in some dark hallway, leading I-don't-know-where.

Then strong hands close, one on each of my shoulders. "Move along. Come on girl. You can do it." He clucks at me, like I'm a horse, and we emerge into a comparatively bright area full of booths with padded vinyl seats, and a serving counter running along one wall, complete with bar stools in front of it.

It's not the family restaurant my dad and Carly's mom brought us to on the first day we were here. The booth seats are patched with duct tape. The cutlery's mismatched. So are the drinking glasses.

I like it.

"Corner booth," Fitch tells me, and drops his hand from my shoulders, and I shiver for just a second, even though it's not cold in here. Even though the closest thing to air conditioning seems to be the three fans whirring into circular blurs against the ceiling.

I wriggle into the very corner of the corner booth, and the seat is soft and comfortable, and the table's at just the right height and distance from the bench, and it smells good in here, and this feeling washes over me, of peace, of relaxation, of quiet, that makes me realize it's been a while since I've felt any of those things, and I close my eyes and breathe in and out, slowly, deeply.

"What?" Fitch's question pops my eyes open, and I'm too chill to spar with him. Too content to bicker.

I stretch my arms out, one then the other, and feel like a cat. "I think I've been tense for a while. It's nice to be here ... where nobody can find me."

"With me?"

"Well, you brought me here, so yeah."

A waitress stops at the end of our table and Fitch turns to her. "I'll have a chocolate milkshake, the Kawartha burger, and lots of fries."

I straighten, "Same for me, but can I also have a pickle on the side? Or, maybe two?" The smell of good food cooking all around us has made the bottom drop out of my stomach. I'm pretty sure I could eat two burgers, but I can't quite bring my-self to order that much food.

With the waitress gone, Fitch turns back to me. "Really?"

I'm slightly faint with hunger. Can't remember where we were in our conversation. "Excuse me?"

"Just, you said it was nice to be here, with me – or at least you sort of said that – but yesterday you said you were happy until I sat down, then you walked away from me. So what is it? I can't keep up with you Tick-Tock."

So, it's not forgotten. I still owe him an apology. I take a deep breath, summon my courage, and say, "Listen, Fitch. That was wrong of me. I shouldn't have said it." I scrunch up my face. "I'm kind of known for saying the wrong thing at the wrong time, but I'm not usually *rude*."

He snorts. "I totally disagree."

"What?"

"You're always rude to me."

I lean forward to protest, but he's still talking.

"It's great. I love it. I ..." The waitress slides our milkshakes onto the table, and Fitch takes a deep sip of his before continuing. "Do you have a brother?"

"Yeah ..." I let my voice lift – let it say *why on earth do you want to know that*?

"My brother's gone," Fitch says. "To university on the west coast. I never see him anymore. He used to give me such a hard time; but in a funny way. He's so smart – my brain can never keep up with his."

Fitch has been studying the smooth chocolate surface of his milkshake, but now he flicks his gaze up to meet mine. "I miss it. You're the first person who's pushed back on me since he left. Talking to you reminds me of talking to him."

It's my turn to sip at my shake. Everything about this afternoon has surprised me. Fitch bringing me here. This heart-to-heart about his brother. And it's just weird to be away from camp after not leaving the place for what's only been just over a week, but feels like forever.

I feel like Fitch has told me something important about himself and, like one of those Choose Your Own Adventure books, I can react in so many ways; all with different outcomes. I can be compassionate and interested. I can share a deep meaningful story of my own. Or I can keep doing what he says he likes about me; pushing back – making fun.

In the end I do what comes easiest to me – I open my mouth and say the first thing that comes to my mind.

"So, are you saying you think of me like your surrogate brother?"

His laugh is sudden, short, and sharp. Just like his mother's. It's the first real similarity I've seen between them ... other than the mobile eyebrows.

"Yeah, that's it. My brother." He wrinkles his nose and his eyes sparkle. "Except you don't stink."

"Oh-kay. Thanks. I think."

We both sit back as our burgers are placed on the table.

"No, seriously, you have no idea. That guy's feet reek. I'm giving you a massive compliment."

"My feet don't stink, but other than that I'm like your brother. Do I have that straight?"

Fitch takes a bite of burger, chews, swallows. "Pretty much."

"Good to know," I say. "Very useful information."

⟨⟨⟩⟩

Fitch and I are behind the Julianne Hills van on the way back to camp.

It's rush hour in Julianne – meaning a single car is crossing our path through the flashing-light intersection – so we stop behind the van waiting for the coast to be clear.

There's a familiar halo of curly hair against the back window.

"Uh-oh," I say.

Fitch drums the steering wheel with his long, strong swimmer's fingers. "What?"

"That's Carly." I point.

"So what?"

*Oh.* Good question. Why don't I want her to see me?

"Well, you know, we share a room. It's not in my best interests to make my roommate jealous."

We're moving now – accelerating to follow the van. Fitch glances at me for a second. "Ah, yes, I hate it when girls fight over me."

*Crap.* The good food and break from responsibility have lulled me into letting my guard down. I should know better by now than to hand Fitch that kind of ammo.

I cross my arms. "The Jeep."

"Pardon me?"

"She'd be jealous because – while this isn't exactly the nicest ride ever to come off an assembly line – it smells much, much better than that van."

"Hmm ..." Fitch slows as the van's brake lights flash red. "So that's it? It's about the Jeep?"

"Absolutely."

"Well, that's pretty lame." He leans on the horn. I snatch for his hand, pull it away, but he finds the button again and gives it another long blast. Then he shakes his finger at me. "You should know better than to interfere with somebody when they're driving."

Before I can say anything, he points forward. "Oh, look. Seems like – what's her name? Carly? – seems like she's seen you."

Carly's got her nose pressed to the back window of the van and has both her palms up, eyebrows lifted.

Fitch lifts his hand and gives Carly a little wave. Then he turns to me. "Sorry. Hope she doesn't put a frog in your bed or anything. But, you know, if it's just about the Jeep, I'm sure you'll be fine."

〈※〉

I'm standing in line in the dining hall, waiting for what looks like it could be our best meal yet – breakfast for dinner, with all-you-can-eat pancakes and even a few measly strips of bacon – when the hard edge of a tray bumps into my back.

"What?" I whirl around to face a grinning Carly. "Ow! That hurt!"

"So did seeing you in a cute guy's cute car instead of slumming it in the big white van with me."

I rub at my back. "Yeah, that. Did you get lots of candy?"

Carly sets her tray down to transfer a platter of pancakes onto it. "Oh, no. Do you think you can just change the subject that easily? What's up with you and Fitch?"

I shiver. Me and Fitch. Not that I'd admit it to Carly, but it sounds kind of nice ...

I concentrate on keeping my features even. "I wouldn't get too excited if I were you. He was my back-up rider for my hacks this morning, and then he offered me a lift into the village because I remind him of his brother."

"His brother?"

"Yeah who apparently, has horrifically smelly feet."

"He told you that?"

"Yup."

She sighs. "That's disappointing." Then she grabs a pour container of maple syrup and brightens. I think she's just excited to have the syrup until she says, "Unless he's just covering up, and he actually likes you, and doesn't know how to tell you!"

My heart thumps a little, and I don't even have any syrup yet.

Then Carly shakes her head. "Except it would be a pretty weird way to your heart – you know; comparing you to his brother. Definitely odd."

She shakes her head. "That's really too bad; it would have been fun to have a camp romance to follow."

"Says you," I say. "I think I probably just dodged a bullet."

We walk back to our tables side by side and Carly hip bumps me. "Don't worry Lacey. One day you'll be in love with someone just as much as Cade and I are in love."

*Ugh.* If I could pick a bullet to dodge, it would definitely be Cade, and any future mention of him. Fitch, on the other hand ... well, I'm not sure if I'd take a bullet for him, but I think I might have already been hit by cupid's arrow.

Which, to quote Carly, could prove to be quite disappointing.

# Chapter Twelve

———

Forget feeling out of place in the diner in Julianne. Forget feeling self-conscious in Fitch's Jeep. Forget the fact that I'll probably never feel quite right in the thin, creaky, bunk bed that sways alarmingly when Carly gets in or out of her bottom bunk.

Forget the dodgy food, and my insecurities about teaching riding.

When I duck through the rails and cross the paddock to Night, and when he pushes his muzzle into my hands and blows out warm air, and then he follows me back to the gate without me even snapping the lead on his halter, I'm home.

All I need to be at home is a horse I love.

I talk to him while I groom him, because it settles me and I hope it settles him, too. Hope he's not thinking "Man, she's got a grating voice. I wish she'd shut up."

I giggle. "Is that what you're thinking, boy?"

Then I giggle again. "But I guess you never know what anyone's thinking because, apparently, Fitch thinks I'm just like his brother. Ha!"

When I told Karen I was going to ride Night today, she helped me hunt out tack that would fit him. "How about Apple's bridle – it's got a nice, thick snaffle – and Drummer's saddle should fit, plus it's comfortable to sit in, and I'd use Mickey's girth."

Night's calm while I put all this gear on him. You wouldn't think he hadn't been tacked up in a year. Then again, I take my time – *no rush, no rush, no rush* – and I adjust straps as I go, and do my best to make sure it's all comfortable; nothing's rubbing, nothing's too loose or too tight.

As I lead him to the sand ring, part of me feels like there should be somebody here watching me, just in case. But I don't want to wait, don't want to rely on other people. Plus, Karen knew I was going to ride him this afternoon, and I left a note on the whiteboard in our cabin: *Carly, riding Night this evening. If I'm not back by lights out I'm probably trampled in the sand ring. Bring help. :)* The happy face was to show her it was a joke. Kind of.

I just can't bring myself to be alarmed by this horse. To me, he's the embodiment of calm. His pretty ears flick around, taking in the sounds around him, but he never pins them. He moves his big, expressive eyes – I swear he even twitches his horsey brow, just like Fitch. Maybe that's why I feel comfortable around him.

I close the sand ring gate behind us, just in case, pull down my stirrups, gather up my reins and use one of the cavaletti blocks to mount. Lay my weight across his back, with both legs free behind me, so I can just kick out and slide to the ground if I need to.

Night swings his head around and pokes at my side with his nose as though to say, "I've never been ridden like this before."

Well, what the heck? If I'm going to do this, I might as well do it properly.

I swing my right leg over his back – careful not to bump,

scrape, or startle him.

Once I have a leg on each side of him – once I'm settled deep in the saddle and my heels are down, with my legs hugging the outline of his barrel without gripping – a sense of belonging washes through me.

Some horses you just fit. Right from the beginning. It was like that the first time I got on Salem. My elbows bent in the right place, so my hands rested at the right spot. The width of her barrel, and the length of my legs was just right.

It's the same with this horse. He's right for me. I'm right for him.

He's waiting – not tense, just patient – and when I think *walk*, he walks.

He's bendier than I expected. Like a rubber band. Even as unfit as he is, he's lean and muscular – a huge contrast from Declan's sturdiness on this morning's hacks.

Night carries himself, and he carries me. I scratch his withers, and he arches his neck, and I say, "How could anyone not ride you for a whole year? What were they thinking?"

Maybe it's because I didn't have high expectations, and I don't ask for much. Maybe it's because it's been a long week and I'm tired and relaxed. Maybe he's just a really, really, truly, great horse. Or maybe it is some mystical thing – some *clicking* – destiny of some sort, but he really doesn't put a foot wrong. At least, I don't feel like he does.

We walk; that's all. I try to mix it up – lots of turns, bends, and circles. Serpentines and changes across the diagonal. We walk up the quarter line, up the centre line. I think of leg yielding, but then think *no rush*. Next time. We can do that next time.

Right before I finish riding him, I ask him for a trot, and he jumps forward, eager and reaching, with the power of a horse a hand taller than he is springing me out of the saddle with each step. Once around on the right rein, once around on the left, and I ask him to walk again.

I lift the saddle off his back right in the sand ring, and his coat is slightly wet underneath. Just enough to show me it was work to carry me today – it was an effort to go through his paces – but it clearly wasn't terribly hard work.

Then I pull his bridle off too, and turn to hang the tack on the rails while I let him have some free time in the sand ring.

Fitch is standing there.

"Hey! What are you doing here?"

"Watching to see if you crack your head open riding a horse nobody's been on for a year."

I clap my hand over my heart. "Oh, Fitch. I'm touched."

"I told you. My brother's gone. I'd die of boredom if I didn't have you to talk to."

"Careful. I'm going to start thinking you care about me."

He sniffs. "Our insurance coverage sucks. We can't afford it if you fall off and sue us."

I nod. "Now that's starting to sound more believable."

While we've been talking Night has been circling, circling, hanging his head low and sniffing the ground. I reach out, grab Fitch's arm. "He's about to go!"

And he does. His front legs buckle and he collapses; losing all his grace in the awkward, jerky movements he uses to lower his whole body to the ground, then lurch himself backward and forward, letting the sand scratch all his itchy spots, grinding his muscles into the dirt.

The missing grace is replaced by joy, though. I turn to Fitch, smiling. "What makes you that happy?"

He doesn't hesitate. "Swimming ... in fact ..."

"In fact what?"

"In fact, try not to bug me too much and I'll take you to the best place to swim in the world. The secret swimming hole my brother and I used to go to all the time."

"Where is it?"

I've been too enthusiastic, though. He laughs. "Good, I've got something you want. Now I can hold it over your head. I'll show you when I'm ready. When I'm sure you're worthy."

I shrug. "Suit yourself. As if I really care anyway."

He laughs. "You want to know. I can tell." He pushes away from the rail. "Your horse is done rolling. Since I now know you haven't suffered a concussion, and won't be initiating a lawsuit against our family, I'll leave you to take care of him."

I watch him go. He's right. I do want to know where the swimming hole is. I also want to know why a guy who rides like Fitch, and is surrounded by horses every day, all the time, picks swimming as the thing that makes him happiest.

Maybe it's just me, but it seems weird.

# Chapter Thirteen

---

B y the second week of camp I'm in a rhythm. My body's used to getting up early to traipse out to the field with Karen and bring in the herd. It's also become accustomed to eating my biggest meal at breakfast – filling up on Corn Flakes and Rice Krispies, and, if I can, hoarding a banana for later in the day – and then eating progressively less as the meals become more complex and less edible.

My riders learn something every day. In fact, they learn something every lesson, which means they learn something twice a day. I'm starting to think we'll actually have something to show their parents by the end-of-session horseshow.

I hardly see Carly anymore, except still asleep in her bed when I drop to the floor as quietly as I can every morning. The calendar hanging on the wall beside her bunk has big black Xs marching toward the final day of the session – horseshow day for me – and both the Saturday and Sunday have huge pink hearts ballooning out of them.

I have the same calendar in my head, except instead of hearts, my weekend holds lists.

*People / Animals:* Salem, Jessie, Meg, Jared, Dad, even Will. Oh, and the seven kittens my dad emailed me to say the barn cat had two days ago. Cade? Am I thinking of Cade? No, I'm too busy. Besides, I'd say Carly's got the market cornered on thinking about him.

*Places / Things:* The ferry, the river, my own bed, hay fields, Jared's barn.

*Food:* Anything cooked by my Aunt Jane, a pie made by Betsy, Nanaimo bars from the bakery, anything I want out of the fridge, whenever I want it.

I see Miranda every night. It's mostly down to the two of us, digging into the freezer, chatting and laughing while we eat our ice cream at the picnic table with her watching her cabin door, and me quelling the growls in my hungry stomach.

I hardly see Fitch. At all. But he does hand his iPad off to me a couple of times. It lets me receive a welcome email from my university telling me, as a scholarship winner, I'll be getting a single room in residence. Reminding me of when I'll need to pay my fees. My chest tightens, but I clap my hand to my breastbone, force myself to breathe through it. I've paid my deposit and I'm earning money every day that I'm here. It's OK.

Halfway through the week Meg confirms she and Jared will come to pick me up. We'll be there right around noon on Saturday. We can take you out for a late lunch if there's a place nearby that you like.

My mind flashes to sitting in the diner across from Fitch. It already feels like so long ago. It was good. I'll get Meg and Jared to take me back there.

Fitch has been good to me. Fitch took me to that diner. Fitch loaned me this iPad. I sign out of my email and pull up the Notes app on his iPad.

Type Thanks … brother :) so it'll be the first thing he sees next time he uses the tablet.

◇◈◇

Night is great, too. I thought I'd give up my free time in the afternoon to ride him, but there's a good reason we don't ride between 1:00 and 3:00; it's just so, so hot.

Karen's been fine about me staying behind after my evening lesson, and it's better for Night, as riding unfit as he is, to work then, when the sun starts to lower toward the treetops.

The first couple of days I strode out through the paddock to catch him. There's a corner, where the grass grows particularly long, and I'd find him there, with his long forelock sweeping across his face, strands poking out of the corners of his mouth.

On the third day he was waiting for me at the gate.

My heart swelled. No horse has ever done this for me before. Not even Salem. I mean, she'll come if I call her, and there have definitely been times when she's been grazing near the gate when I've gone to ride her, but Night is clearly waiting, ears pricked, head over the top bar.

The fourth day he whickers and, a shot of pure joy runs through my core, lightening my heart, and my step, and lifting my shoulders.

"Oh buddy, boy. Oh sweet, sweet baby." Nonsense talk, but he seems OK with it. I babble as I smooth brushes over his ever-shinier coat. As I dig out twigs, and leaves, and burrs, embedded in his not-brushed-for-a-year-tail. As I bit-by-bit even the ragged ends of his long-neglected mane.

The forelock I don't touch, though. It's too much a part of him. I braid it in a long, fat braid, and tuck the tapering end under the brow band of the bridle so he can see when we work in the ring, but I always finger comb it long and loose again before I turn him out.

I don't know if it's that I'm relaxed, or exhausted, by the

time I ride him, but I'm loose. I should probably have my reins shorter. Should maybe introduce more structure into our sessions, but I'm too – again; relaxed or tired? Not sure.

The fact is, it's working for us.

I've already cantered him on both reins; finding the gait is as rocking-horse smooth as his trot is jarring. I'm getting used to the trot, though. It forces me to be disciplined with my posting, and I experiment with truly using my rising as a proper aid in a way I never have before. I leave the reins alone and concentrate on shortening and lengthening his stride using the tempo of my posting alone.

It's exciting when I start to be able to feel a clear difference. I scratch his withers, "Good boy!" and, like I always do, bring him back to a walk while he's still just lightly sweating. He can already work a bit longer – a bit harder – before getting to that point. Progress.

I feel like my summer is about progress in baby steps. Gradual improvement with my riding students. Careful advances with Night. Slowly earning money for university.

That last one is painfully slow ... but it's happening.

The temperature edges up all week. Each day it's one or two degrees hotter than the day before.

Fitch makes himself even more popular with the campers by adding an extra hour of free swim squeezed in after the last riding lesson and before turn-in time.

Friday morning, when I tip-toe out of the cabin into the early-morning mist, it's already twenty-six degrees.

In my morning lessons we practice riding into the ring, lining up, finding space on the rail, smiling for the judge. All at a walk. Just a walk. The horses' saddle pads are still soaking when the girls untack them. The girls' hair is plastered to their heads when they take their helmets off.

"No riding this afternoon," I tell them.

"Then what instead?" Ava asks.

"Baths."

"For us, or the horses?"

I laugh. "You'll see – they'll be for both of you. Don't wear anything you can't get wet."

And so the afternoon is wet, and fun, and I'm not sure if the horses end up cleaner than when they started, but the girls are satisfied – convinced they're ready for the show tomorrow – and that's all that matters.

Because it's the last night of camp, dinner is pizza. Real honest-to-goodness pizza, delivered from the village, and I eat like a pig. I make up for all the dinners I've skipped all session. I'm already looking forward to the next Friday-night-before-the-end-of-session pizza dinner in three more weeks.

I don't ride Night – just bring him in, groom him, and free lunge him a bit. When I turn him back out I whisper in his ear, "I'm going home tomorrow ..." my stomach does a quick twist-untwist at being able to say *tomorrow*, "... so you just chill, rest, think about what we've been working on, and I'll see you Sunday."

When I sink onto the steps in front of the cabin, and unlace my paddock boots, the screams, and shouts, and splashes from the pool carry clearly across the common. So free swim's still on.

I smile, tuck my dusty boots against the railing; one flopped over from the ankle, the other sporting one grommet much shinier than the rest, where I had to get the shoemaker to re-place the original one which tore out.

I wriggle my toes into my flip-flops, turn the bottoms of my breeches up to leave my legs bare below my knees, and walk over to the pool.

It takes about thirty seconds of standing on the pool deck for my ears to even begin to adjust to the din. These girls are sugar-and-carb-loaded. After pizza they had make-your-own sundaes. There was a new flavour of ice cream – Rocky Road – I'm thinking of having some tonight.

They're horseshow-nervous, and going-home excited. They're in making-the-most-of-our-last-night-at-camp mode.

They're wild.

"Hey!" Fitch has to stand so close for me to hear him, that I more feel the word, than hear it. Warmth on my neck; vibrations in my ear drum.

And something else. A tug, a pull ... I can't place it. My mind roams to Cade – the last guy who stood this close to me. The *only* guy who's ever stood this close to me. But, no, that's not it ...

Before I can figure it out, Fitch grips my shoulder and takes one big step back toward the poolhouse. I go with him, and the noise level drops by a few decibels. He points at the pool. "Don't suppose you want to go in?"

I shake my head. "Not a chance! Not with this mob ..."

"I really need to show you that swimming hole," he says.

I cross my arms in front of me. "Promises, promises."

"Yeah, well, if you weren't ditching us ..."

I poke at my ribs. "I need to go home to store up some calories."

"Lightweight!"

I nod. "Exactly what I'm trying to tell you!"

"When you get back," he says.

"What if I don't come back?"

For just two seconds he takes his eyes off the pool and trains them right on me. "Oh, you're coming back."

There it is again – that feeling – the one I can't put my finger on. Warmth spreading. Everything else dropping away. "I ..." I shake my head, break his gaze. "I should let you work."

"Unfortunately, you're right." He bumps my shoulder with his, and takes a step forward, back into the wall of noise, and I'm left to walk back through the pool house, walk back across the commons, listen to the sounds of the pool fading behind me, hear the sharp whinny of one of the horses to another ...

I inhale, so sharp and fast, I suck a bug in and choke.

The horses. Their whinnies.

I know where I've had that feeling before. The one I get when Fitch is an inch or two inside my personal space.

It's the feeling I got when Night whickers to me.

It's bliss, and joy, and happiness, and belonging.

I pinch my wrist. It's me, being in for big, big heartache if I'm not careful. *Shit.*

"There's something ..." Miranda pauses, spoon in the air, nose lifted, scenting like a horse does. Her eyes meet mine. "Don't you think? There's something in the air?"

I take an exaggerated sniff. "Yeah. Like cigarettes."

Her brow furrows. "I don't like those three."

The three counsellors, she means. Ponytail-peach-schnapps and her posse.

"You think it's them?" I ask.

"Who else?"

She's right. It's not us. It's not Carly – coaxing and pleading with the staff computer. It's not the other counsellors who we've invited in the past, but are too timid to raid the ice cream tubs with us. If you won't steal ice cream, there's no way you'll leave your cabin full of campers and hide up somewhere to smoke.

"They'd better not be smoking near the barns." I shudder.

Miranda scowls. "They shouldn't be smoking anywhere around here. If we can smell it, the kids can smell it." She shakes her head. "It's not just the smoking either."

"What do you mean?"

She digs deep into her ice cream and pops a loaded spoonful into her mouth before answering. "You don't see it, because you're at the barn all day, but when we do stuff in groups – when the campers are together – those three just plunk their kids down and huddle up. They're always whispering. It's been getting worse all week."

She licks her spoon. "You know when I went back to the kitchen last night?"

I nod, she'd taken off her hoodie to scoop our ice cream, and ended up forgetting it.

"Well, when I came back out of the kitchen, I heard an engine. I walked down the drive a bit, and there was a car, just past the big house. The inside light was on, and ponytail was sitting in the passenger seat next to some guy."

"Who?" I ask.

Miranda shrugs. "Who knows? They all live around here – I guess one of their boyfriends, or brothers, or cousins ... it's just ..."

"Not quite right," I say.

Her eyes meet mine. "You said it, exactly. It's nothing I can put my finger on – nothing I'm about to take to Jan – but it's not quite right."

"Hmmm ..." I scrape up the last melty bits of my Rocky Road. "Well hopefully the break will help. Let's see what things are like when we get back."

# Chapter Fourteen

---

"Lacey! My stirrups won't budge!"

"Here, Ava, let your legs hang down." I squint to see where the irons are hitting in relation to her ankle, snick them up a hole, and say, "You can't just *yank* like that – it makes them stick – pull out instead of down."

"Lacey! I forgot the order of the paces in the class."

"It's fine, Sarah. Just listen to the judge. She'll tell you what she wants, and she won't ask you to do anything you don't know how to do."

"Lacey! My hair!"

"Oh!" Rebecca's hair is a mess. It's sticking out from absolutely every gap possible in her helmet. I take her horse's reins. "Hop off."

I look around for someone to hand the reins off to. "That's my mom." Rebecca points at a woman holding up her cell phone, snapping pictures.

"Here." I hold the reins out to the woman. "Can you please hold him just for a minute?"

Rebecca's slightly overweight horse immediately lurches his head for the grass. "Hup!" I flick his bottom lip. "None of that!" I slide Rebecca's mom's hands up the reins, close to the bit. "If you hold him here, he won't try to get away with that."

Rebecca's mom's wide eyes make me think I don't have that much time before she lets go of the horse, so I whip the girl's helmet off, finger-comb her hair, then smooth it with my palms, whip a quick braid through it – secured with a braiding elastic – and fish a hairnet out of my pocket.

What does it say about my life that I have hairnets in my pockets? I'm trying not to think about it ...

Rebecca's hair does look a million times better when I snug her helmet back in place, though, and her lovely clean grey mount doesn't have any green grass foam around his mouth, so disaster averted.

It's weird to stand outside the ring, and watch my riders ride, and just do ... nothing. Just smile at them, and focus on their improvement, and realize the small mistakes really don't matter – not at all – and hear their parents ooh and aah, and call their names – "Hey, Ava sweetie – looking good!" and take pictures of them.

There's an actual outside judge for the day, and she pins ribbons on the girls who've ridden particularly well – a few who came into camp with some riding already under their belts, but a couple who have worked hard, and improved immensely.

As the novice division winds down, I go to the middle of the ring where Jan hands me a microphone and I give a little speech about how great and rewarding it's been to teach everybody's children, and I give fun and silly awards like, "Best at scrubbing out manure stains," and "Most likely to sweep up for a friend," and then my riders take their horses back to the barn, and untack, and groom, and I supervise, but also talk to parents who pull me aside and say, "Thank you," and "She looks so happy," and I'm surprised that, in some ways, I really wish they weren't all leaving today.

I mean, yes, I want the break – that's for sure – but I'd pick up again with my little groups in a heartbeat. At this point it would definitely be easier than starting with a whole new bunch of kids ... that's a chest-tightening thought and I'm trying to avoid those, so I skip it.

And then ... I'm done.

My bag's packed – ready before I went to bed last night. My bed – which I won't come back to until Sunday – is made. Every one of my campers has a parent with her.

The staff all got our phones back after breakfast this morning, and I read a text from Meg saying, On 10:00 boat. Can't wait to see you!

I do the mental math I've done my whole life – other kids know times tables; island kids know ferry timetables – and figure out they'll be here ... *soon*. Wow. In maybe half-an-hour. It's hard to believe.

I head back toward the show ring to watch the more experienced riders while I wait. One of my campers runs over with a box of Timbits and I score a chocolate one. "Take another one!" she says, so I grab an apple fritter, too. Yum.

I'm one foot up on the fence, clapping at the right times, still tasting the donut holes, but dreaming of another diner hamburger, when my arm's jostled.

"Hey." Fitch looks immensely presentable – if I'm honest, immensely *handsome* – wearing a polo shirt with Julianne Hills embroidered over the left side of his chest, and non-surf shorts. Shorts with a belt, that look like they might have been ironed.

I raise my eyebrows, make a show of looking him up and down. "No wonder it took you so long to show up. Have you spent the morning getting ready?"

"Is that your way of saying I look nice?"

I laugh. "You know what I love about you? Your modesty."

"It's not me saying I look good, Tick-Tock, it's the admiration in your eyes."

*Crap. Must hide that better.*

I snort in as non-admiring a way as I possibly can. "So, this is the kind of stuff you used to talk about with your brother?"

He goes still. Clears his throat. Am I imagining it, or is the great, super-cool, always-unruffled Fitch Carmichael going ever-so-slightly pink in the cheeks? If so, it makes him look really cute. *Stop it Lacey!*

"What?" I finally ask.

"It's just ... about that brother thing ..."

"Yeah? What ... Oh! My! God!" Over Fitch's shoulder I catch sight of a face that sets off fireworks of joy in me. Buzzing, fizzing, popping, exploding ... I didn't know how much I loved that face, how much I missed it until now. "I ... oh ... Jared!"

I sidestep, and Jared steps forward, arms out. "Hey, pretty girl!"

Then I'm in his hug, and I'm pressing my face as tight as I can to his chest because – oh, so embarrassing – but I'm crying. Crying with relief, and happiness, and a sudden realization of how tired I am, and how great it is to have the person here – the *people* here; because Meg's standing to the side, beaming, and I want to hug her too – who will look after me for the next twenty-four hours.

And I want them to meet Fitch. I've felt his presence off to my side the whole time I was greeting them. While Meg squeezed me and said, "Oh, Lace, it is so good to see you, and I'm so proud of you," I was loving it and, at the same time, counting off the seconds in my head until I could open my body and say, 'I'd like you to meet Fitch.'

When I finally say it, lifting my voice to start, "There's someone I'd like ..." I turn, and he's gone.

The presence I've been feeling is nothing – an empty space. How stupid do I feel?

"What?" asks Meg. "A friend you wanted to introduce us to?"

"Um, yeah. I guess he had to go."

"Well, we still need to pick up your things. Maybe we'll catch up with him before we go?"

I smile. "Maybe. You're right. Let's get my stuff so we can have lunch. I'm starving!"

I know Fitch won't be anywhere near my cabin, but it doesn't stop me looking as I pass my bag to Jared, and show Meg my tall, creaking bunk. I slow my steps as we walk past the pool, making sure to point it out to Meg and Jared. No Fitch. As we coast down the driveway, my gaze lingers on the house, but it's as quiet as always, with no visible activity.

I half-expect Fitch to be seated in the diner when we walk in. How cool would that be? He could share our booth with us. Meg and Jared would like him – I know they would.

By "expect" I really mean "wish." He isn't there just like, deep down, I knew he wouldn't be.

But it is great to tuck into a huge burger.

And it's fantastic to climb into the backseat of Meg's little car – I turn down Jared's offer to let me ride shotgun – "No thanks; I think I'll just stretch out back here."

With my stomach full, and the sun pouring through the windows, heating the interior of the car, and the highway humming under the tires, and no responsibilities for twenty-four hours, I fall promptly, and deeply asleep.

I half-wake when the car slows and the tires *bump-bump* with a metallic clang under us. I hear Meg say to Jared, "Well, that never happens," and I half-register that we've driven into line and straight onto the waiting ferry.

I almost wake up all the way when Meg shuts off the car engine but, within seconds, the huge ferry engines take over, humming, thrumming, white-noising me back to sleep, and it's only when we drive off on the island side that I sit up, and yawn, and stretch.

It's a good thing I napped, because I have so much to fit

into such a short time.

It's perfect to be back. Almost. Because Salem's still unmistakably off. But she's Salem. She's sweet and sunny, and she nuzzles me for carrots like always, and we run and play in the round pen Jared built for Meg, and when I'm with her it's like I was never gone.

I tell Meg about Night while we groom Salem together, and with Meg, too, it's like no time has passed.

"I'm surprised how much I like teaching," I tell her. "I thought I'd be too impatient. I didn't think I'd know what I was doing."

"Let me guess," she says. "You're figuring it out as you go along."

I straighten Salem's forelock – so tame and tidy compared to Night's – and blow my own hair out of my face. "Yeah, I guess I am. How did you know?"

"Because I've watched you all these years. Working with Salem. Working with the other horses we've had here. That's your strength. You're good at it."

"If I'm good at it, it's only because you taught me."

Meg laugh, hooks her arm around my shoulders. "Aah! Mutual admiration lovefest!"

I grin. She's right. That's what Meg and I do. Boost each other up. Adore each other. Never say a bad word about each other. And it works for us.

Just like, weirdly, the complete opposite – insults, and teasing, and giving each other a hard time – works for me and Fitch.

*Fitch.* The tiniest of shadows crosses my perfect afternoon.

Whatever. I'll see him tomorrow. I need to enjoy this, today.

〈⦻〉

The perfection-imperfection continues. Jared's mom – my Aunt Jane cooks a massive meal for us. Meg and Jared are there, of course, and my dad and my brother, and Betsy and Carl, who Meg used to work for. There's lasagna, and there's salad, and there are three kinds of pie, and Betsy hands me a tightly-wrapped lemon loaf – "To take back to camp with you," she says. "Just in case you need a snack."

Snack? This will be lunch for the foreseeable future.

After dinner, Will and I do the dishes – I wash; he dries.

We're silent at first and it's not an easy silence.

I try to break it by asking him about Bridget.

"She's fine," he says. "It's kind of hard with her staying in Toronto this summer but, you know, she's really happy there." He shrugs. "I guess I'm just supposed to sit around here and work all day long while everyone else goes off and does what they want."

When he says "everyone," I hear "you." My blood pressure spikes.

My fingers are pruning up, and there are still far too many dishes left. Will dumps a glass he deems insufficiently clean back into the sink. Irritation's starting to spark my brain.

I'm so close to snapping back at him. Telling him to grow up; stop being such a crybaby, spend a day doing what I do – eating what I eat – and see how he likes it.

But the set of his jaw tells me he's just as irritated as me. I don't have long at home. I don't want to spend it fighting with my brother.

"How's the tractor?" I ask.

There's nothing Will likes talking about more than farm equipment, and there are few things I find more boring.

His face lightens and he doesn't hesitate. "Ever since Jared gave it that overhaul, it's been running so quietly it sounds like a Prius."

"Like a Prius, huh?"

He takes a glass from my hand, meeting my eyes as he does so. "You don't really care, do you?"

I grin. "I do care." I shake a stray strand of hair out of my face. "OK, maybe not about the exact details of how the tractor runs, but I care about what's happening here. I care about you. I miss being here you know, Will."

He takes a good long time drying the glass, then sets it down. "We miss having you, too. It's pretty quiet without you around."

I keep my voice casual. "Well, I'm glad the tractor's running so well. It sounds like it should last a while longer."

"Yeah, and now Jared knows what's wrong with it, so he could probably fix it again."

I stream the worst of the water off a heavy glass dish and hand it to him. "One less thing to worry about."

He accepts it from me. "True enough."

Then, in the ultimate peace offering, I say. "If you want to tell me about the combine, I'll listen."

# Chapter Fifteen

---

My time on the island goes too quickly. I knew it would, but I didn't know it would be for this reason.

Didn't know I wouldn't really start to feel at home again – feel easy in my surroundings – until noon on Sunday. Pretty much when I need to think about leaving again.

"Your mom wants you to have dinner with her," my dad told me last night as we drove home from Aunt Jane's.

I guess it's not a surprise. I mean a mother wanting to see her daughter is a pretty normal thing. My mother and I, though, have never really had a "normal" relationship. Still ... not going to see her could be the first step in tipping our relationship from distant to hostile, and I can do without that.

My dad can do without that while the divorce arrangements are pending.

So, my dad and I drive onto the 4:30 ferry to give me a little time to visit with my mom before eating an early dinner and getting back to camp. Meg rides the ferry over, too, but she isn't getting off. She'll just take it back again and spend the evening with Jared.

The thought gives me a twist in my throat. It's a beautiful,

beautiful, island day, with the sun glinting off the wavelets in the harbour, and the wind turbines ticking over lazily in the unusually light breeze. The sunset tonight will be gorgeous, the bird and insect songs will be loud and melodic with no wind to drown them out, and I want to be staying.

I also want to be eating good food with somebody I like, who likes me. Want to be close enough to somebody to feel that fluttering behind my breastbone, the race in my pulse, the breathlessness that makes everything more fun, exciting, and intense. I imagine walking in the just-cut hayfield, holding hands, being pressed against the warm, round bales. I imagine his breath on my neck, his teeth catching my earlobe, and his strong, swimmer's hands going around my waist, pulling me tight.

There's no more room for Cade in my fantasies. It's all Fitch. Fantasy Fitch is a million times better than real-life Cade. Which is unfortunate, because he is – you know – a *fantasy*.

"Have I lost you?" Meg asks.

I sigh. "No. I just ..."

I look at her familiar face, at the smile that tells me she's waiting; ready for me to tell her whatever I want to ... and I chicken out.

Instead I ask, "How did you get together with Jared?"

Her eyes widen. "You were there that summer, Lace. You remember."

"Well, sort of. I mean, yeah, I know how you *met*, but he wasn't your boyfriend right away. And you guys weren't exactly sharing all those details with me at the time ..."

She laughs. "I guess not." Her eyes focus somewhere in the distance. "Well, I guess there was this spark right away ..." Her mouth curves up at the corners. "We had this stupid inside joke about his tractor – I thought of him as 'tractor guy' – but I hadn't had a boyfriend before, and I didn't know how cool and *rare* it was to be able to talk and joke with someone like that, and so ..." She gives her head a tiny shake and looks straight at me. "I took too long. I should have just kissed him right away. Much sooner than I did, anyway."

"Did you think he was good-looking?"

"Of course I did. Still do. I think he's gorgeous." She lays a hand on my arm – sorry, I know he's your cousin. "But it was deeper than that. There are, possibly, guys who other people would think are better looking, but I was attracted to Jared from the beginning. There was like a magnet making me want to be close to him, and when I was ... when I am ..." She gives a little shiver.

I hold up my hand. "Hmm ... yeah ... cousin alert."

But I get what she means. Totally. In fact I had to damp down my own little shiver listening to her words, thinking about Fitch.

I'm big on taking Meg's advice. It's always worked for me in the past. But it's also always been about horses. I'll have to think about her whole 'I should have just kissed him right away,' statement. I'm not sure if I'm brave enough for that one.

My mom's new house is, well, I always stare at it for about ten seconds before I move to open the door of the truck. It's not the circular driveway with the fountain in the middle. It's not the three stories of solid limestone, or the roof clad in real-honest-to-goodness slate tiles. It's not even the sun-silvered lake in the backyard.

It's all of those things together. And the red convertible parked at the side of the driveway just ahead of us. And the shiny pick-up, so monstrous it dwarfs my dad's old pick-up. With personalized plates that read MR HAMR.

Really? "Mr. Hammer?" So can my mom look forward to being Mrs. Hammer?

I just can't believe my mom could need or want anything from my dad – from the farm – when she has all this. But I guess *she* doesn't have any of this. It's Mr. Hammer's. Or Sonny. My mom explained that's what I'm supposed to call him because his real name's Robertson Findlay the third, but there's no way he'd get any respect from the construction crews who work for him with a name like that, so everyone just calls him Sonny.

It's also why he drives the pick-up, and not the Jaguar convertible. The little sports car is strictly for Sunday drives with my mom, or the weekend trips they take to wineries in Prince Edward County, or musicals in Toronto.

Sonny's walking across the driveway now. Big smile on his high-cheekboned face. Arms open to meet me as I step out of the truck. "Lacey! We've been excited to see you!" He hugs me, and I hug him back. How can I not? Sonny's nice. Kind. Well-intentioned. Happy. "We know you don't have much time at home and we're so happy you could come."

My dad's out now, too. Standing on the gravel beside me. "Rod!" Sonny extends his arm, pumps my dad's hand. "Will you stay? Can I get you a beer?"

"Thanks," my dad says. "No. I have a couple of errands to do. I'll come back to pick Lacey up later." He coughs. "Is, uh, Maddy here?"

"Oh yes. Of course. Just, putting on the finishing touches, you know?"

"Oh yes. Of course." I wonder if my dad knows he just echoed Sonny's words. Something about him – his face just a little too straight; his hand tapping his thigh – makes me think it was probably on purpose.

"Did you need to talk to her?" Sonny asks.

"Oh no. Just making sure ..." He doesn't finish but he doesn't

have to. We all know no father should really have to say "...
that she's going to be here to have dinner with her daughter,"
but we all know the idea that she wouldn't be isn't completely
unfathomable.

I follow Sonny into the round entry hall framed by a gently rising round staircase leading to a second floor I've never been to. I'm glad he tells me not to take off my flip-flops
because even on this hot July day I feel like the marble floor
would be cold underfoot.

My mom's sitting on the sheltered stone patio built with a
prime view of the lake. She's not putting finishing touches on
anything at all, except maybe the martini in her hand, but she
is here, so points to Sonny for that.

"Darling! I would get up but ..."

"Don't be silly." I lean forward and kiss her cheek. "It's me.
No need."

I got my height from my dad. I was taller than my mom
when I was eleven.

I got my strength from my dad – my long bones, and sinewy
muscles, and the habit of working them from sun-up to sun-
down when necessary. Which, on a farm, is often.

I got my quick temper, my difficulty meeting strangers'
eyes, and my tendency to tear up at a sad song, from my dad.

Of the things my mom had to give; a breathtaking singing
voice, a light step and ballerina grace, and the ability to turn
every head in a room, I got none. There's more of her in Will.
My brother can sing, and when he does, everyone listening is
mesmerized. Back when she was my best friend, Bridget told
me it was one of the things that first made her fall for Will.
"When he picks up that guitar, and opens his mouth, Lace,
you just want to be the girl sitting next to him."

She's humming now – my mother – one of the simple, out-
ward signs of her happiness. Sonny, and his lifestyle make her
happy. I'm happy for her – happy for all of us – when content,

my mom is a joy to have in your life. Unsettled, she attracts, creates, and spreads drama. Long may Sonny make her happy, and long may she give him joy.

Sonny has the best barbecue money can buy, and he knows how to use it.

He grills chicken because he remembers I liked it last time I was here. He produces a salad he made earlier. He served delicious fizzy lemonade when Will and I ate here a month or so ago, and I drank three then, so he has half-a-dozen cold bottles in the outdoor fridge.

"Thanks Sonny," I say. "It's a great dinner."

My mom beams. "Isn't he wonderful?"

The meal stays pleasant because Sonny asks me about camp, and I tell him about raiding the ice cream freezer, and how terrible the beds are, and then I ask him about his latest project and, even though construction isn't necessarily my thing, he's super-enthusiastic and it's easy to listen to somebody talk about something they love.

And then my mom starts talking.

This is when it becomes clear my mom hasn't been listening to our conversation, because she doesn't wait for an opening, or even make a faint effort to segue her thought into ours, she just says what she's thinking – what she wants to say – and we're supposed to stop talking and let her.

She sets down her drink and says, "Now, Lacey. Have you considered going to university here like I asked you to?"

"Mom, I decided a long time ago where I was going to university. I've already accepted, and paid deposits, and that's why I'm working at camp – to pay for it."

She flutters her hands. "But that's the point Lacey. If you'd stay here, you wouldn't have to pay for anything. For goodness' sake, there's a building named after Sonny up on campus; they're hardly going to charge his stepdaughter tuition."

I'm grateful when Sonny steps in. He tops up the wine

my mom's been drinking. "Now Maddy, that building's not *quite* named after me. And Lacey's not my stepdaughter ... yet ..." He smiles at me. "Although that would be lovely, of course."

She laughs. "Oh Sonny, you're so proper. That's what I love about you. So it's named after your father, or grandfather, whatever – your name still carries weight there and we all know it's a fantastic school. Lacey would be getting a world-class education."

"Maddy, she has to do what she wants. She can't study agriculture there." He turns to me. "I'm proud of you for working for what you want Lacey. You made a choice and you're making it happen."

Sonny has to be careful because my mom's sighing and twirling her hair around one finger. Just because her new boyfriend is "wonderful" doesn't mean he can't annoy her. She leans forward, places both hands flat on the table and rolls her shoulders back. "Lacey I know you're determined – you come by it honestly; I've never met anyone so stubborn as your father – but I have lived longer than you, and I do know a few things. This is a great school, you'd learn so much here, and it would take all the financial pressure off you. You don't have anything to prove by working all summer at that camp, you know. We all get that you're a hard worker. Why don't you just relax and let yourself enjoy the rest of your summer?"

I tell myself I'm not even considering her offer because I really, really want to go away to school – it's what I decided, and I'm sticking to it. And that's partially true, of course, but also I can't imagine not going back to Julianne Hills. Not with Night knee-deep in his grassy paddock waiting for me.

Not with Fitch ... well ... whatever Fitch is to me – I pinch my wrist to give myself a dose of reality – probably nothing, but I'll never know if I don't go back.

"Listen, Mom," I say. "I appreciate what you're saying. It's generous, and I can see how it makes sense. But I've made a choice. You've made some choices this last little while, and they make you happy, and I'm happy for you. I'm just asking you to be happy for me."

She takes a deep breath, and I have no idea how this is going to go.

She pushes her lips together. "Oh Lacey, you're such a smart girl, and you like to take your own path. You got those things from me, so I have to admire them ..." She claps her hand to her chest. "You just don't know what it's like to be a mother. I feel things so strongly for you. I just want what's best."

*Oh lord.* It's hard not to think of all the times everybody else's mom volunteered at school, and mine didn't. Or when she had a fight with her sister on Christmas Eve and declared "There's no way I'm setting foot in that witch's house," and my dad bundled Will and me into the car and drove us across the province to take us to see my mom's family – his in-laws – so we could have Christmas with our cousins. Or, over the last few years, at every single horse show and event, where always Meg, and sometimes Jared, and often my dad, stood on the sidelines, but no mom, of course.

But she believes what she's saying. In her mind she wants what's best for me. So I bite my tongue. "I know you do, Mom."

The doorbell rings, and I understand the exact meaning of being saved by the bell. Oh. Thank. Goodness.

"That's Dad. I'd better go."

"Shall I ...?" My mom half rises, but I shake my head. "That's fine, Mom. I can make it to the door by myself."

Sonny does get up. "I'll walk her out, Maddy."

She beams. "Thanks babe. Could you bring my wrap back with you? I'm getting a little cold."

"Of course."

Sonny walks by my side. "She does want you to be happy."

"I know."

"I think it's easier for me to see things objectively, since I'm not your parent. I think you're making a good decision. I'll try to reassure her."

I stop and turn to him, my eyes sweeping the opulent décor around me. If Sonny had been my dad I could be going to university anywhere in the world, and not worry about working to pay my tuition.

But if Sonny had been my dad, I can't imagine I'd be wanting to go away to study agriculture.

So I guess I should just be glad that Sonny's my - nearly - stepdad and he definitely makes the time I spend with my mother easier.

"Thanks for everything, Sonny."

And he walks me out to where my dad's waiting by the truck and stretches his hand out. "Hi Rod. Had a great dinner with your daughter. Thanks for bringing her ..."

It's time to go.

⟨⟨⟩⟩

It's getting dark when we pull into camp. My dad carries my bag in for me; gives me a hug.

Carly's not back yet. Our small cabin is empty.

I don't want to watch my dad drive away, but I can't not.

It's bittersweet, standing on the rickety porch, watching his taillights disappear.

I was really just home long enough to miss it. But out there, in the dark, is Night and I'll see him soon. And scattered through the cabins all around me are the new campers who will be in my riding groups tomorrow, and - who knows

– maybe I'll grow to like them just as much as I liked my first groups.

And beyond the tall post shining a pool of light on the common area, past the pool, just down the drive a little, well ... I'm not actually sure if thinking about him is a good idea.

After all, I want to get some sleep ...

# C h a p t e r   S i x t e e n

---

"I hope this works!"

I'm already more relaxed. Less worried about what my students will think. They love horses – or, at least, they're supposed to; that's why they're here – I love horses, so if I show them what I love about horses we should all get along fine.

"Have any of you ever heard of joining up with your horse?"

Of the six girls perched on the fence surrounding the sand ring, two put up their hands. And only about halfway. So, they're not quite sure.

I've used jump standards and rails to cut the sand ring in half. This is as close as we're going to get to having a round pen to work with.

I lead Bugsy – a chunky dappled grey pony to the middle of the ring. "We're going to see if Bugsy's ever heard of joining up!"

Something about starting this way with Night – taking just a bit of time to get to know him; to let him know me, before jumping into riding him – made me think I should do the same with my campers. Riding is about more than just sitting on a horse's back and steering, but if I don't take the time to show them that, how will they ever know?

I slip Bugsy's halter off, and he gives me the suspicious look of an entrenched school horse who was resigned to doing more work than he wanted to, but now finds himself loose in a sand ring. The flicking of his ears asks me 'What's up with this?' and 'Why are you letting me go?' and 'Is there hard work involved for me?'

I turn to the girls. "I'm going to talk you through what I'm doing, and I want you to pay attention, because the main thing I'm doing is showing Bugsy he can trust me."

I pick up the lunge whip and give it a flick, and Bugsy gives his head a shake and moves out onto the rail, and we've started.

I talk the girls through every step and, even though I probably look like I know what I'm doing, I'm still a little shocked that it all goes according to plan. Within half-an-hour the tough old school horse is following me around like a dog.

As I slip the halter back on, in preparation for leading Bugsy back into the barn, I tell the girls. "I'd like you to keep this in mind when you ride. You can't all do this exact exercise with the horses you'll be riding here, but you can respect them, and earn their trust. You'll enjoy your riding more, and be better riders if you think of your horse."

For the final fifteen minutes of their lesson time, I get the girls to take each of their assigned horses into the aisles. "Groom them. Talk to them. Get to know them. You'll ride them this afternoon."

As the hour ends, Ava comes up to me. "I'm so happy to see you back," I tell her.

She smiles. "I was supposed to go to gymnastics camp for the next three weeks, but I begged my mom and she let me come back here."

"Well, I'm glad," I say. "You'll be so good by the end of this session that you can move up to the intermediate group."

She shakes her head. "Oh no. If that happens, I'll go to gymnastics camp." She points at Bugsy. "That was so cool."

"I'm glad you liked it."

"No other riding instructor would ever do that," she says.

I don't know if she's right, and if she is, I don't know if me doing it is a good idea, or just silliness, but it's what I've decided on, so my morning is filled with two more join ups and more encouragement to the riders to get to know their mounts.

As I'm giving the aisle a final sweep, getting ready to go to lunch, Jan appears in the doorway. "I saw what you were doing out there."

I hold my breath. Prepare to say sorry. Prepare to defend myself. Wonder which I should do.

"Interesting," she says. And then she goes.

Warm breath tickles my arm and I turn to the horse sticking his nose out of the nearest stall. I rub his muzzle and say, "Yeah, I know. Weird, right?"

Then I head for lunch.

There was no Fitch at breakfast, and there's no Fitch at lunch. Carly's there, though, with a starry look in her eyes. She tells me five times, "It was just *such* a great weekend."

It's clear she wants me to ask for details; she's itching to spill them, but I just can't do it. Which makes me feel petty, because wouldn't a true friend say, "Oh yeah? Tell me about it."

But I can't. I can't listen to bliss and rapture about Cade and true love while I walk around with butterflies flinging themselves at the inside of my stomach wondering *Where is Fitch?* And *When will I see him?* And *What will I say?*

I can't eat, and it's not even the fault of the food, which is fine today. Grilled cheese sandwiches. Hard to screw up.

I'm done lunch ten minutes before afternoon activities start so I head straight to the pool house. None of the campers should be here yet, but I'm hoping Fitch will be.

I've got my bag of shower stuff with me as an excuse, even though I came back to camp clean last night and I haven't done much to get dirty yet. I'm hardly desperate for a shower. But I am desperate to see Fitch.

The slap of my flip-flops echoes in the cinderblock hallway leading to the pool. I step out onto the pool deck and even though he should be here, and I came expecting him to be here, my stomach still does a crazy somersault when I see he really is here, at the far end of the pool, holding the skimmer, looking taller, fitter, and more tanned than he did forty-eight hours ago when I last saw him.

"Hey!" I call.

He looks up from the pool surface. "Oh. Hi Lacey."

I laugh. "Well, that's a first."

"What is?"

"You calling me 'Lacey.' I didn't know you actually knew my name. What happened to Tick-Tock?"

He pushes a lock of hair out of his face. "Yeah. That was kind of stupid. I'm sorry about that."

This is wrong. This is stiff. This is like a totally different person in front of me. He told me he liked our insults. Told me it was fun. So I keep trying. "Wow! If you're going to apologize for every stupid thing you've said to me we'll be here for a long time."

His eyebrow lift, which I'd come to quite like before now, is arrogant and dismissive again. Probably because his eyes are flat and he's not smiling. "I didn't know I was that bad. I'm sorry if I insulted you."

"What are you talking about Fitch? What is up with you?

I've been looking forward to seeing you ..."

He clears his throat. "Listen, I can't really talk anymore." He juts his chin past me; toward the entrance to the pool deck. "The kids are arriving. So ..."

"So ... what?" I ask. "So, later?"

"Of course. I'm sure I'll see you later."

"I ..." I look at him. I wait. But he's giving me nothing. I feel like I've been slapped. Like I've been dumped in the deep end of the pool without knowing how to swim. I feel like crying, but I smile instead because now there are ten little girls on the deck and I teach some of them, so "Hey girls!" I say. "Have a great lesson!"

And I go.

I'm embarrassed. I'm humiliated. I'm confused. I'm a little bit angry. And I'm very sad.

So I head for the paddock. Off to see the guy I know will be waiting for me, and happy to see me, and who will have a special whicker just for me.

The heat wave broke when camp did, and while it'll definitely stoke up again before too long, the temperature's still quite cool with no humidity.

I decide it's high time I took Night on a hack and, even though it's mid-afternoon, today is cool enough to let me do it.

His walk is swinging and forward, head held at attention, ears always flickering ahead, back, side. To me, to the sounds of the fields around us, to the whinny of one of the other horses back in the paddock.

I think again that it was a crime for an animal this inquisitive to be left in a field for a year.

I also find it hard to believe any rider would want to abandon him. Nothing about working with him so far has been difficult.

I mean, sure, he's spirited, and energetic, but he's not a runaway, or nasty.

Maybe he and his rider started off on the wrong foot. Maybe she just really didn't like riding that much. Maybe he's matured in the year since she left him here.

*Maybe, maybe, maybe.*

Maybe Fitch figured out I like him, and he's avoiding me so he doesn't have to deal with it. Maybe he decided I wasn't as funny as his brother. Maybe he has a girlfriend who found out he'd been lending me his iPad and she told him to stop.

*Maybe, maybe, maybe.*

"I'm not supposed to be thinking about him, right bud?" I scratch Night's withers, and he twists both his ears back to me for two seconds before one tunes into birdsong, and the other sweeps the area for any other important sounds.

The trails here are nice. I have to admit it. And there's extra challenge added by the hilly terrain. As we work our way around the side of the large hill behind the camp, the trails turn to twisty, dirt paths, more overgrown than the network I led my campers along last session. We trek up and down frequent small rises, and I'm often shifting my weight to reduce the effort Night has to put out to carry me. At one point we step out of a narrow passage between trees and my jaw drops. Just across from us is a ski hill.

It's small but complete, with a chairlift running up between two well-defined runs, cut out of the thick trees covering the rest of the hillside.

There are lights on tall poles strung up alongside one of the runs, and a building at the base of the lift. I bet this place is hopping in the winter.

Not now though. It's strangely quiet. I'm not much for

post-apocalyptic stories, but I've read one or two, and this is the first real-life example I've seen of a place built for people, now abandoned – even if only seasonally. It's kind of eerie.

Night shifts under me. "You think so too? Let's head back."

Whether it's his own instinct paralleling mine, or my creeped-outedness trickling through to him, he nearly trips over himself to turn around, and his walk back is rushed – head bobbing – verging on a trot.

Night doesn't slow until we're back on the wider trails, closer to the camp. Covered with tanbark, and carefully trimmed of all branches hanging into the riding space, it feels like we've come back to a paved highway after being on a bendy dirt road.

Although Jan does save money on certain things – like decent mattresses and quality people food – I have to hand it to her; she definitely puts the horses first. They eat, sleep, and work in safe, well-maintained surroundings.

Before long we step out into full light in the wide-open expanse of the big cross-country field facing the sand rings, arena, and barns. Even though I know much of the schooling-horse tack is patched, and the tractor's been overhauled more times than the one we use at home for haying, from here the spread is impressive; neat and prosperous. No wonder wealthy people ship their expensive horses and precious daughters here to ride.

My chest swells just a tiny bit. I teach here. Maybe this place isn't so bad.

I glance at my watch. No shower, no iPad, no nothing means I still have a good amount of time before I have to teach. There's a narrow indentation worn around the perimeter of this huge field – a conditioning track. Staying at a walk in the shade of the trees has kept Night from breaking a sweat. I decide it's a good time to start work on his fitness.

I point him counter-clockwise on the track and squeeze my

legs, keeping my hands light. He steps into a trot and I sit deep in the saddle, driving with my hips, keeping my legs on. His strides lengthen, and we move quickly past the trees. We eat the ground to the first corner and I support him through it before asking him to lengthen again on the next straight side.

I ride him around the entire outside of the field, maintaining a forward, working trot, only bringing him back to a walk when we cross the spot where we started our circuit.

His nostrils are slightly flared and his neck is damp. He's worked, but he's nowhere near tired-out.

That's good. I'm satisfied. I let the reins slide long and loose, stroke his neck, and let him pick his way across the field back home.

〈⊗〉

Something's happening. That feeling of a brewing storm from last week – the one I thought was about the intensifying heat and humidity – well, when I get to dinner it's clear it hasn't broken with the weather. The three-musketeer counsellors are more thick-as-thieves than ever. They've actually re-arranged their campers' seating so two of their tables are made up entirely of little girls, while the three of them sit together at the third.

"Can they do that?" I ask Miranda when we're both at the front picking up food for our tables.

She shrugs. "Who's going to stop them?"

I scan the room. It's a good question. Jan's not here. And, of course, if she isn't, neither is Owen.

My gaze continues until I spot Fitch standing near the door. I absolutely did not expect to see him here. He never comes for dinner.

My body does a whole bunch of disconcerting things at

once. My heart stands still, then revs. My mouth goes dry, and my hands go clammy. I shiver, then heat washes through me.

"Lace? You OK?" Miranda's nudging me.

"Uh, yeah. Fine. Just trying to figure out what this meat is."

I look at her for a second, look at the mystery meat for a second, then I have to look back at Fitch.

I'm not the only one who's spotted him. Number three – not ponytail, or acne, but the one I've always found less noticeable ... until now ... weaves her way around tables until she's by Fitch's side.

He's quite tall, and she's very, very small – cutely so? – I've never wondered before, but I do now.

She stands on her toes and puts one hand on his arm, cups the other one around her mouth while she says something very close to his ear.

Those eyebrows of his fly up.

I suddenly hate the girl I've never noticed before. Hate the sparkly Juicy spread across the bum of her too-tight sweatpants. Hate the criss-crossy fitted yoga top she's wearing, displaying a mis-matched mess of tan lines. Hate the tattoo on her shoulder.

The corner of Fitch's mouth tugs up. To me, he's not looking enough like he hates her.

She says something else before dropping down and stepping away from him. I can see her face, and she gives a wink. I follow the wink to ponytail, sitting back at their table, winking back.

I. Am. Going. To. Be. Sick.

That thing ponytail said last session about Fitch picking a counsellor and getting what he wants floats back into my mind. I didn't think much of it; it didn't sound like the Fitch I knew. Maybe that was the problem. Maybe I was so clueless I didn't understand what was really supposed to go on between Fitch and me. Maybe he got fed up of me not catching on, so he's finding someone who will.

Seriously. Ill.

I still don't think Fitch is really like that. Or maybe I just don't want to think so.

I glance back at Fitch and he's staring at me. My body runs through the dry / clammy, hot / cold cycle all over again, and I'm too busy trying to deal with that to do anything smart like smile, or wave, and God knows what expression he reads on my face, but it's clearly nothing that makes him want to stay. He looks away, and turns and walks out the door, and if I thought our meeting at the pool was as bad as it could get, I was definitely wrong.

This is stupid. I should go after him.

I mean, we were good, we were great. We were pals, we were brothers-from-another-mother.

And nothing bad happened, so we should still be those things, right?

That reasoning gets me as far as setting my tray down and heading for the door. I'm going after him.

Except.

It's true we didn't fight. It's true there was no incident. But ever since that moment where I turned to introduce him to Meg and Jared, and he was gone, there's been a sliver of ice in my heart. An edge of not-quite-right in my brain.

I'm still following Fitch. Pushing through the double doors. But my stomach's churning.

Because this time last week, if he'd spotted me in the dining hall like he did just now, he wouldn't have missed the chance to come over and insult me about something. About not finding him earlier. He would have said something about sending out a search party, or it being nice of me to finally turn up, or asking if I thought I was too good for him.

But tonight, nothing. A look and a walk away. What's up with that?

My feet hit the path outside only about a minute after his. He should be just ahead. Once I round these bushes, it should be easy for me to spot him; to catch up with him.

And I'm just going to ask what's going on. If something's wrong. And he can tell me not to be so silly, so sensitive, such a girl.

My fingers are crossed as tightly as I can hold them together. It's a habit so old I can't even remember when I started it. If I keep them crossed he'll be walking on the path just ahead of me when I get past this big bush in *three-two-one* ...

No Fitch.

He's not ahead of me. He's nowhere in sight. Which, since this is the shortest way to his house – to everything else in the camp, really – makes no sense at all.

Unless he thought I'd follow him and wanted to make sure I wouldn't catch up.

I turn back to the dining hall. I don't know if I'm right or wrong. Paranoid or perceptive.

I just know there's nobody I want to talk to more than Fitch right now, and I'm getting more and more worried my chances to do that are over.

# Chapter Seventeen

---

By the time we head for ice cream I'm over-tired, over-hungry, and over-analyzing every single possible tiny aspect of everything I've ever said to Fitch, everything he's ever said to me, and the scary unknown things Juicy-tattoo girl might have whispered to him in the dining hall.

"You guys owe me one!" Miranda says. "I found the ice cream order sheets and I added Chocolate Chip Cookie Dough to the next order."

"Awesome," I know it's the right thing to say, but I really couldn't care less if she'd added Corrugated Cardboard ice cream to the next order.

Carly, meanwhile, will not shut up.

In self-defence, I start counting how many times she says Cade's name. When she gets to twenty-six, I stop counting for fear I'll hit her, and she'll be the one using actual self-defence on me.

Cade was sweet. Cade was amazing. Cade was waiting at her house when she got home on Saturday. Cade bought her flowers. Cade sent a care package back to camp with her.

*Cade, Cade, Cade.*

Carly's standing right next to me, waiting while Miranda scoops our ice cream, and the overpowering fruity scent of the gum she's chewing is making me slightly queasy.

I wrinkle my nose. "That gum was in the care package, right?"

She gives a couple of extra-quick chews. "How do you know?"

"Oh, his breath smelled like that when ..." *Shit.*

I didn't mean – I really didn't ever mean – for Carly to know Cade kissed me. I just have no filters tonight.

At least I stopped before I actually said it, but from the looks on both Carly's and Miranda's faces, my sudden silence is just as bad as what I nearly said.

"When, *what*, Lacey?"

"When ... just whenever he's been around I've noticed it." I wave my hand in front of my face. "It's a pretty strong smell."

"That's not what you were going to say."

I look at Miranda. *Help.* Her eyes are wide.

"It is what I was going to say. I'm just tired tonight Carly ... kind of out of it. It was just a throwaway comment. It was nothing."

"Now, I know ..." Carly breathes.

"Now you know what?" I ask.

"He asks about you sometimes. At weird times. I just thought he was trying to be nice – show an interest in my friends." She pauses, locks her eyes on mine. "When did you sleep with him?"

"Oh my God!" I drop my still-unfilled bowl. "I didn't sleep with him. It was just a stupid, tiny, nothing kiss ..."

Carly's eyes widen. "I never thought you slept with him, you idiot. I didn't think you kissed him either, but now I know you did!"

"Wait! Carly ... *I* didn't kiss *him*. It wasn't like that. And it was way before you got together. It was back at the beginning of June, at the pork roast at Ellie Liselot's house ..." I taper off. Why am I still talking? The tears filling Carly's eyes tell me I'm only making things worse.

"How do you know we weren't together then, Lacey? Huh?" She bends over, wraps her arms around her stomach. "I think I'm going to be sick."

*Because he kissed me.* That's how I always thought I knew they weren't together yet. But I'm starting to see how maybe that was a false assumption.

*Oh crap.*

This is bad. I think of how I felt watching Juicy-girl flirt with Fitch, and he isn't even my boyfriend. Carly must feel ten times worse.

And, small matter, but she currently sleeps in a bed underneath mine, and the over-her-shoulder look she throws me as she stumbles out of the kitchen door, tells me when she stops crying, she might want to kill me.

"Oh. My. Wow." Miranda is standing, looking at the door, then back at me. If she hates me too, I'm sunk. If she won't talk to me that'll make Fitch, and Carly, and Miranda. I might as well move out to the barn. I might as well sleep in the hayloft.

Miranda shakes her head. "Well, he sounds like a major skank."

I laugh. Against all odds, the relief flooding me sends laughter coursing through me. It's my turn to clutch my stomach, and giggle, and shake, and collapse against the freezer, and slide to the floor. Once I'm sitting down there, and the hiccups hit, Miranda crouches down beside me. "So, what next?"

I gasp for air. "I feel like someone should go after her."

Miranda sighs. "But, clearly, it shouldn't be you."

"Probably not."

"OK. You watch my cabin for me, I'll go find Carly. And try to talk to her."

"Thanks Miranda. I owe you one."

She shrugs. "It'll get better. Eventually."

This time last week I would have done anything for a break from the heat, but as I sit on the steps in front of Miranda's cabin, I wish it was a bit warmer.

The late night, my lack of sleep, the dipping nighttime temperatures, and my general sense of gloominess have me wrapping my arms around myself.

When Miranda and Carly finally appear, relief fights with worry.

Good, they're here. Carly hasn't jumped off a bridge, or hitchhiked into town to catch the first bus home.

Crap, they're here. I have to sit here while Carly walks past me.

I guess she's tired, too, because she doesn't take a swipe at me – verbal or otherwise. She just walks straight by, eyes on Miranda's door, and pushes inside.

"She's going to crash on my floor tonight," Miranda says.

I nod. "Yeah. Thanks. That's probably good."

I'm not even going to think ahead to tomorrow morning, and noon, and evening, when Carly and I have to share the same dining table. Not even going to imagine trying to sleep stacked above her bunk – the wall behind it speckled with pictures of Cade, and notes from Cade, and a wisp of paper from a fortune cookie he gave her reading, You will soon get unexpected kisses in unexpected places.

I just rise to my feet, my cold knees creaking as I straighten them, and head back to get a few hours' sleep before I have to bring in the herd.

# Chapter Eighteen

―――――――――――――

Breakfast.

No Fitch. No Carly.

Well, not exactly true. Carly sits at a table of one of the quietest counsellors of all, who has a spare seat at her table after one of her campers was sent home yesterday with chicken pox blooming on her skin.

Carly doesn't look at me once. To me, even her back looks angry.

My morning lessons go surprisingly well. It's like being persona non grata everywhere else, makes me work hard to be extra loved in the barn. I'm nurturing, patient, and helpful to my riders. I talk them through their problems. I give them the benefit of the doubt.

When one girl cannot get her pony into the corners, and I know, yes, he's taking advantage of her, but no, she's not trying hard enough – I give her a break. "Bring him here."

I climb on, and it's bizarre to have my legs spread wider than they are on the much-bigger Salem or Night, but to be so, so close to the ground. Pony physique. This guy sure wouldn't win a swimsuit contest.

It takes one trot down the long side, with him mouthing

the bit, and his ears zoned on me, for him to decide it's not worth fighting me. He bends deep into each corner, and when I ride him back, all the little girls ask, "How did you do that?" and I have a momentary flashback to being thirteen years old myself, and watching Meg climb on my fat pony, Cisco, and make him go perfectly. I think life was simpler then – all I was worried about was Cisco – and wonder why I had to grow up and get a more complicated life, and tears sting the back of my eyes, but I smile and say, "Alyssa's going to get on him and do it now, and you'll see it's something you can all do."

Lunch.

No Fitch. Carly still on the other side of the dining hall.

Today I do need a shower. When I go the pool area's abandoned because wind and rain have blown in, with movies in the dining hall substituted for swimming lessons.

With the rain still drumming down on the barn roof, it's bandaging and wound treatment for all my riders. They all try making spider bandages and giggle when they slide off their horses' legs.

The only good thing about dinner is catching a couple of my students wrapping each other's legs with polos they must have smuggled from the barn. I don't tell them off. I'm just pleased to have done something somebody likes.

After my evening lesson – more bandaging – I walk back from the barn with water dripping off the edge of my raincoat hood. It's such a dark, dark night. No moon, no stars, nothing but rain falling from the sky, and puddles underfoot.

I don't want to go back to the cabin I share with Carly. It's too small to be shut up inside with somebody who despises me.

I want to be loved, and understood. I want someone to make me laugh.

I really, really, want Fitch. Fitch-from-last-session. Mean-but-funny-Fitch. I'll even tamp down my crush on him – tell myself I don't like him like *that* – handle it if he's decided he likes Juicy girl and that's why he's been avoiding me.

I at least want him to be my friend.

I walk to his house.

Which is so incredibly not-helpful because what on earth am I supposed to do there?

I'm guessing one of the bedrooms upstairs is his, but I have no idea which one. And even if I did, what am I going to do? Stand in the rain and throw pebbles at his window? As if – this isn't a movie. I'd a) miss the window, b) break the window, c) get it wrong and hit his mother's window. A shudder runs through me.

So, I'm going to have to fall back on my ring-the-doorbell-for-a-manufactured-reason-and-hope-Fitch-answers    ploy. Not that I've had wild success with it, but I've got no pride left; I can admit I'm desperate.

OK, so what's the made-up reason?

I still haven't decided when I mount the steps to the door.

I'm worn out, brain-fuzzed, can't be smart, can't be clever.

The rain's pouring down on my head, and I'm waiting for inspiration to strike, when Fitch walks into the porch, eyes down. He must be looking for something.

I breathe in so sharply I hiccup. I've lost all feeling below my knees.

*Do it Lacey!*

I lift my hand and rap my knuckles on the glass.

Now I think I've made Fitch hiccup. A start jolts his body and his eyes fly to the door. He's squinting as he walks up to the glass, shading his eyes, trying to see into the dark.

When his eyes meet mine he goes still.

It's like a switch flips in me. I go from being sad, to being mad in two seconds flat. "Oh, for God's sake, let me in!"

I don't know if he can hear me, but he can definitely see my lips moving and read the expression on my face. For a split second, I'm convinced a smile tugs at his mouth. If so, it's gone right away, but the possibility of it having been there makes me bold.

He opens the door. "What are you doing ...?"

I step in. The first thing I do is grab a baseball cap – one I've seen Fitch wearing before – from a hook next to me.

He starts again. "What ...?"

"Shut up!" I whisper it with a hiss in my voice.

He opens his mouth.

"I said 'shut up!'" I stamp my foot. "*You*, are being a total jerk to me. I want to know why."

He opens his mouth again, and I put my hand up, palm toward him.

"No, actually, I don't even care why. I just want you to stop."

A fat drop of rain plops off my hood onto my nose. "Do you know why I want you to stop? Because on top of all the usual things like never having food I can eat, and no privacy at all, and getting up really early, and only finishing work ..." I look at my watch. "... now – when it's getting dark." I take a deep breath. "On top of all those things, now Carly – my *roommate* who I have to *live* with – isn't talking to me, and I don't have her, and I don't have you because you're icing me out for some unknown reason, and it really, really sucks, and I've had enough of it."

"Lacey ..." Fitch starts, but I'm on a roll and I've got to get this all out.

"That was a lie. I do want to know why you're being a jerk, but I can find out later. For now I just want my friend back. I want you back. And the way you were a friend was by being a jerk to me, so that just shows how pathetic I am. I want you to be mean to me."

I wait. He doesn't say anything.

"I'm done now," I say. "You can talk."

Maybe getting all my anger out wasn't such a good idea.

Now I'm just left with a hollowness inside me, filled with nothing but butterflies.

What if he tells me to go? What if he doesn't say anything at all? What if he just gives me more icy politeness?

He crosses his arms in front of him, and tilts his head. "How mean do you want me to be?"

"Oh!" Relief swamps me. A nasty Fitch is a good Fitch.

I want to jump up and down, want to hug him, but I can't, because Jan is stepping into the hall behind him.

I hold out the baseball cap. It's wet. I've been letting my raincoat drip onto it. "Here. Like I said, you should be more careful. I found it in a puddle on the road."

His brow furrows, nose wrinkles, then his mom takes another step and his peripheral vision catches her. "Oh. Yeah. The cap. It's funny. I didn't think I'd left it out there."

"Well, obviously you did."

"Hmmm ... yeah, obviously."

"Fitch!" It's the most expression I've ever heard in Jan's voice. "You're not being very gracious. Please say thank you to Lacey."

He blinks twice, fast. "Thanks, Lacey."

I lift my chin. "My pleasure."

He takes the cap. "Wow, this is really wet."

His mom's voice is snappy. "Yes, well, whose fault is that, Fitch?"

"Mine, obviously," he says. "I've been a real jerk lately. I haven't treated my baseball cap properly."

I'm biting my lips. It feels so, so good to have laughter to hold in.

"Fitch, go unload the dishwasher, please. Since Lacey's here, I'd like to speak to her for a moment."

Oh. Hmm. My lifting spirits level out. What does Jan want?

"Lacey, about the join up exercise you did with your groups."

"Yes?" Was that wrong? Did it go against the never-offered-and-one-hundred-per-cent-completely-unwritten-and-un-explained rules of teaching riding at Julianne Hills? Have I screwed up?

"A very interesting approach." Jan nods. I wait for her to add something, but that seems to be it.

"Oh. I ... uh ... I'm glad you were interested."

She opens the door. "Well, good-night. Thank you for bringing my son's cap back. Try to stay dry."

I step back out into the wet and the dark, and I'm still alone, and nothing's fixed with Carly, and it's not like I really had any quality time with Fitch, but I do feel better.

Still not quite good enough to face Carly – which is why I turn my steps to Miranda's cabin – but cheerful enough that I'm actually looking forward to that Chocolate Chip Cookie Dough ice cream.

# Chapter Nineteen

"This *is* good." I turn my spoon upside-down in my mouth, to lick every last bit of Cookie Dough ice cream off it.

Miranda laughs. "Who's amazing?"

I point my spoon at her. "You are."

I take a deep breath. "You are, you know. This late-night ice cream routine has saved me from starvation, and you've been great with this Carly thing."

She shrugs. "Carly will get over it. At least she should. I mean, don't get me wrong, I know it stings, but I think she's smart enough to figure out you're not the instigator here." She pauses. "In fact, I guess you're kind of a victim too. Did you like him? I mean, if he kissed you, then started going out with Carly, did that hurt your feelings?"

Even though the Cade thing doesn't bother me anymore, it's nice to have somebody acknowledge my side of it.

I shrug. "Well, it kind of sucked at first. But I was pretty used to nobody being interested in me, so I just reverted to that when I found out he and Carly were going out."

"Don't say nobody's interested in you."

Miranda's standing next to me – we're eating our ice cream

leaning against the counter because it's still too rainy to sit at the picnic table – and I give her a quick sideways glance, ready to make a flip comment; to brush her off. But her eyes are serious and steady on me.

"You're amazing," she says, and rests her hand on my arm. It's bottom-of-an-ice-cream-bowl cold. A shiver runs up my arm and quivers my shoulders.

Oh. *Oh.* Oh, wow.

"I ... Miranda ... I think you're amazing, too ..."

"But," she says.

"Well, yeah. But I'm not ..."

She squeezes my arm, then lets go. "I know. As if I didn't know. I have eyes, you know."

"What do you mean?"

"Oh, lord! The way you and Fitch stare at each other."

"We don't! I mean, OK, yesterday I kind of stared at him. Yes. But he doesn't ..."

"He does. He likes you. I promise."

"He hasn't spoken to me since I got back to camp." I giggle.

"What's so funny?"

"I went over there tonight. I told him off. I said he was being a jerk and I wanted him to stop. If he ever did like me ..."

"... he probably thinks you're extra-awesome now."

"I think you're delusional Miranda. I think – for some unknown reason – you like me, so you're biased."

She puts her bowl down and steps in front of me so I have to look straight at her. "Here's my question for you, Lace. If I'm not wrong, and he does like you, is that a good thing, or a bad thing?"

I think of Fitch's eyebrows. The tiny scar right in the middle of his chin I've noticed a dozen times, but never managed to ask him about. How I've stopped hearing his insults and mostly just stare at his eyes, and lips, and teeth while he talks.

A fresh tremor runs through me, but unlike the one Miranda gave me, it's warm, and I feel it right through my core.

Miranda snorts. "Uh, yeah, OK. Forget it. Question answered."

# Chapter Twenty

Carly was asleep when I got back from ice cream, and she's not awake yet when I go to catch the herd.

In addition to feeling sorry for myself, I have been feeling sorry for her, as well. I know why she's upset. I just wish she wasn't upset with me.

I grab a pen and the envelope from the card that came in the mail from Meg yesterday and take them outside with me. In the hazy morning light, as neatly as I can while propping the envelope against the cabin wall, I scribble: I'm sorry I hurt your feelings Carly. I hope you're doing OK.

I slide the envelope just inside and pull the door closed gently so it won't disturb the note.

It's not much, but it's true. I don't want her feelings to be hurt.

The balloon of hope I'm carrying around definitely makes it easier to reach out to Carly.

Even though Jan interrupted us, I like the way things ended between me and Fitch. There was ribbing there. There was a return to insults. His mother thought he was being rude to me.

Those have to be good signs.

My gut tells me he's going to come to lunch, and when he does, he's going to sit with me, and I'd better be ready for some major put-downs.

"You look happy," Karen says as she pushes the gate open.

"Hmmm ... yeah. Well, rain's over. No more stable management inside. I can ride Night. It's all good. Right?"

"Sure," she says. "Right. If you say so."

I use pylons, and jump poles, and jump standards, to set up obstacle courses for my riders. There's lots of giggling, at themselves and others, as horses and ponies wander far off course, step on pylons and, especially when a very plump paint pony backs into the box I've laid out on the ground, only to raise his tail and poop.

"Nice!" I say. "Very classy! I was just about to tell you all you owe me a piece of Dubble Bubble from the general store in the village every time your horse kicks over a pylon, but I think a poop on course earns me a Gobstopper as well."

The rest of the morning passes with yells of "Dubble Bubble!" and shrieks of "Gobstopper!"

As I watch my final class finish grooming and settle their horses into their stalls, one by one, I'm bubbling with happiness. Lunch soon! Fitch soon!

I just know it. I just feel it. And Miranda says he likes me ...

I'm humming – I'd be whistling if I knew how – when I do a check into the stall of the final camper's horse to be put away, find his water bucket nearly empty, and unhook it to go fill it at the tap by the side barn door.

"Hmmm-mmm-mmm ..." I turn the tap on, straighten while I wait for the splashing water to fill the bucket, lean against the side of the barn and yell, "Ow!"

The pain is sharp, and searing at first, but the initial shock is already dissipating as I slap my left hand over my right upper arm and stare at the rust-covered nailhead sticking out of the doorframe.

*Well, that's annoying,* I think. *A horse could have really gotten hurt on that.*

I'm not a horse, but my arm is slippery and hot, and when I look at it, there's blood oozing between my fingers.

Oh. Shit. This is not good.

If this *had* happened to a horse, or to Karen, or one of my students, I'd spring into action, but because it's me, my brain goes blank.

It's bleeding quite heavily. As in, running down my arm and splashing into the grass. I can't go back in the barn like this. I'll drip blood on the floor, and the scent will disturb the horses.

"Karen?" I call. "Karen?!?" But there's no answer. She could be anywhere, and the drone of Fitch's dad's ride-on lawn mower is drowning out my voice.

The ride-on mower.

I clamp my hand as tightly as I can over the cut, and start walking toward the sound of the engine.

"Mr. Carmichael? Owen?" I'm an idiot. He's sitting on top of a lawn tractor motor so loud he has ear defenders on. How do I ever think he's going to hear me? But I can't exactly wave my arms around. *Blood spatter ...* I giggle.

*Uh-oh,* I might be getting a little light-headed.

In the end I just eyeball his next strip of grass and go stand there.

I hope he's looking ahead; hope he's paying attention enough to notice a girl, with blood pouring out of her, in his path.

After Fitch's dad cuts the engine, everything happens kind of quickly.

He runs into the barn and comes back with Karen, who's

clutching a shipping bandage and some cotton.

"Sit down," she says. Karen has that experienced horse-woman's way of seeming to have one extra hand than most regular humans. She holds my arm clear of my side, and wraps a smooth, tight bandage at the same time.

"Can you juggle, too?" I giggle.

She frowns. "Are you in shock?"

"Huh?"

"Where are you?"

"At the barn."

"Which barn?"

"Julianne Hills."

"Which way do you wrap a bandage?"

"Tendons in."

"What time of day is it?"

"Nearly lunch ... oh ... it's nearly lunch ..." My arm can't be that badly hurt because I can still feel the pang in my stomach.

"You don't worry about lunch." Karen helps me up. "Look, Owen's here now, with the truck. He's going to take you into town to get stitched up."

I shake my head. "No, I don't need ..."

"Yes you do. Look." She points at the newly snugged bandage and, sure enough, there's a tiny spot of blood already seeping through. She holds the truck door open for me and, once I'm in, laces my fingers through the handle above the door in the truck. "Hold onto that. Keep your arm elevated."

"But what about my lessons?"

"We'll figure it out."

"What about ..."

"What about, what Lacey?"

"No, nothing. Forget it."

Karen shuts the door and speaks across me to Owen. "Get

her something to eat while you're in there, Owen. I'll tell Jan what happened."

Once the hospital staff have determined I'm not actually bleeding out, they leave me to sit and wait.

While Owen goes to get me food, I walk up to the counter. "Should I maybe just leave?"

"Oh no, that cut needs stitches. You can't leave."

So, I can't leave, because I need stitches, but nobody shows any signs of wanting to stitch me up. Sigh ...

Owen brings me a sub, which would normally fill me with joy, but I quickly discover one-handed sub eating is a messy, frustrating, occasionally humiliating, ordeal.

Still, it's better than dining hall food. Except Fitch would have been in the dining hall ... I *think*.

"I'm going to go pick up a couple of things down the street. I'll be back soon. Do you want to call anyone?" Owen hands me his phone.

"Oh. Thank you."

I know the switchboard number at the university by heart. Dial it and asked to be patched through to Meg. Miracle of miracles, she actually answers.

"So, hey," I say. "Don't freak, but I'm sitting in the emergency room."

Then, because I'm bored, and have nobody else to talk to, and nobody's showing any signs of approaching me with a needle and thread, I tell Meg about Carly and me and our fight, and how awkward it is. Which means I have to back up and tell Meg about Cade.

"Why didn't you tell me then?" she asks.

"I don't know. Maybe deep down I knew he wasn't good enough."

She snorts. "He's Olivia Lidwell's little brother, right?"

"Yeah."

"He definitely isn't good enough. You – and Carly, too –

both deserve way, way better than that little twerp."

I laugh. "I guess I should have told you from the beginning. You could have saved me a lot of heartache."

"Just remember that – what else aren't you telling me?"

Outside the emergency room window, Fitch's dad comes into view carrying several shopping bags. "I'll tell you later. I should go now. Can you just tell my dad what happened, but that I'm fine?"

"Of course I'll tell him. And, Lacey?"

"Yeah?"

"You promise you'll tell me whatever you have to tell me later?"

"I promise."

Owen keeps walking. He must be headed for the truck. I look at the phone in my hands. My gaze lingers on the contacts icon. Fitch's number must be there.

My thumb hovers over it, while a battle of call-him-don't-call-him rages in my head.

"Lacey Strickland?" A woman in scrubs stands in the open doorway. She's holding a clipboard and looking at me.

"Oh! Yes! Coming." I palm the phone, and walk to meet her.

She smiles. "Let's get you stitched up."

# Chapter Twenty-One

When Owen pulls the truck into the empty driveway at the house, he grins. "Whoops, guess I'm late."

"Nothing important, I hope."

"No," he says. "Some of Jan's connections from the Business Improvement Area. They have a garden party every summer."

He winks. "It's not my favourite thing, and I wouldn't go, except Fitch'll be there on his own so I should rescue him." He unclicks his seat belt. "Will you be OK now?"

"Of course. I can hardly feel it now. It's just going to be a little inconvenient, and maybe a bit stiff." I rest my hand on the door handle. "Thank you for everything. For lunch, and spending so much time at the hospital. It was really kind of you."

"You helped me miss part of this garden party. I probably owe you."

And, just like that, everything's back to normal.

I get to the dining hall at the tail end of dinner. Just in time to grab a couple of dinner rolls and a bowl of salad that's seen greener, crispier days.

As I'm heading for my table, Carly's heading for the bathroom. "Carly," I say. "Did you get my note?"

She hesitates, then nods. That's all; doesn't say anything, but she meets my eyes for a second. Progress.

I skirt past the table where Ponytail, and Juicy, and the third one sit together all the time now. I glance at them and, I swear, I catch sight of a cell phone in Ponytail's lap.

With their banning during camp time, phones are such a rare sight that they stand out right away. It felt immensely weird to hold Owen's this afternoon.

I double-take, trying to get a second view, but the three of them have closed in; leaning close together, and I can't see anything but their backs.

I know I'm biased, but I still don't like those girls.

〈〉〉

I teach my evening lesson because, why not? What else am I going to do?

After the chattering girls put their horses away and return to their cabins, it's too early to go back to my small cabin and push too hard on the possibly growing truce that might-or-might-not be developing with Carly, so I free lunge Night.

The late-evening light washes over his dark coat, glinting off high and low points – his withers, his flank, the point of his hip – as well as all the new lines and ridges of muscle that have been developing while I've worked him under saddle, and which I can finally see and enjoy now; lunging him without any tack on, standing on the ground and watching him move.

I work on voice commands. Getting Night to move up through his transitions is easy, with the aid of the lunge whip behind my voice. Asking him to move back down requires patience. So. Much. Patience.

I remember Meg's tips. "Always use the same term. So

'walk' is walk. 'Trot' is trot. And so on. Decide what halt is – it might be 'halt' or it might be 'whoa' – but pick one and stick with it. Then, when you want him to move from a canter to a trot, it's not 'whoa,' it's 'trot.' You have to be consistent with him. A trot is a trot is a trot."

She also said my voice should reflect what I want him to do. So to move forward to a trot from a walk, the word should be light and quick – "Trot!" To come back down it should be slow and easy – "Tuh-rot ..."

It takes forever as Night circles at the canter, to get him to return to a trot. When he finally does, I'm sure it's less to do with anything I've said, and more just a natural break in his pace, but I praise the heck out of him anyway.

Going from trot to walk takes even longer because I'm pretty sure he could trot all day. He finally comes down to a walk, though, and I tell him "Good, good boy!"

I get each transition twice, and by then he's been moving in circles around me for long enough, and Karen's leaning over the gate saying, "You've had a big day. You should go to bed."

"I'm OK," I say, but the truth is, my arm's aching so I give in without a fight. "But you're right; he's had enough."

Karen takes the lunge whip from me. "You just turn him out on your way back. I'll put this away."

I yawn long and wide as I head back to the cabins. I don't think there's any way I'm going to make it until ice cream time tonight.

Our cabin is empty when I get back, and I remember there's a movie in the dining hall tonight – figure Carly must be there – and think maybe it's just as well anyway, as I make an awkward hauling, bumping, one-armed climb up to my bunk and flake out.

TUDOR ROBINS

Night's biting me. Right on my arm. It hurts but I know he doesn't mean it. He's agitated because Jan is trying to take him away from me.

She can't. I love him as much as Salem. I can't lose him now.

Jan's holding my hand; trying to pry it from Night's lead shank.

*No, no, no ...*

"Lacey!"

"No ... I won't ..."

"Lacey! You have to get up. Lacey, come on."

Oh my arm. It really hurts.

I blink and focus, not on Jan's face, but Carly's.

"Carly?"

"You have to get up. Fitch is at our door."

"Fitch? Why?"

"You tell me. He wants to see you."

"I ... OK." The painkillers they gave me at the hospital must have worn off. My cut's throbbing in what I suspect is the same rhythm as my heart beat.

"Are you up?" Carly asks. "Because Miranda needs me. I've gotta go. I need to make sure you're getting out of bed."

"Yeah, I'm getting up. See?" I slide to the floor as she pushes back outside.

*Fitch.* Carly said Fitch. What am I even wearing?

Who cares. It's not like I'm going to change. Fitch's outline is visible against the screen door. He's right there.

My heart speeds up, and I forget the pain in my arm.

I pull the screen door open and step outside. "Hey, what are you ...?"

He cuts me off. "Are you OK?"

"What? Yeah, of course."

"My stupid parents. They didn't tell me. It was only on the way home from that dumb party that my mom asked my dad if you were OK. I can't believe he just dropped you off here alone. I can't believe my mom still went out."

"I'm fine, Fitch."

"You were in the ER. All afternoon."

"It's just a cut." I lift my sleeve. "Some stitches."

He sucks in his breath. "Lacey, that looks horrible."

I glance down. I guess it kind of does. It's the stitches that make the slash across my arm look angry, sore. And the skin around it is starting to bruise.

But I was lucky, the doctor said. The nail didn't tear anything important. And my tetanus shots are up to date. He pretty much filed it under 'could-have-been-much-worse.'

"Does it hurt?" Fitch asks.

"Well ..."

"It does. Oh Lace." He lifts his hand to my shoulder, then just skims the cut – not even touching it, but I can feel this kind of forcefield put out by his hand warming my arm. Warming all of me, actually, from the inside out.

And it's just like Meg said; there's a kind of magnet pull. I'm afraid to look in his eye because when I do I won't be able to look away.

I breathe deeply, and he can see my nostrils flare; swallow, and he can watch my throat ripple.

I'm vulnerable. I might as well say, "I like you, OK. I really, really, like you."

Having it be so obvious is embarrassing and exciting at the same time.

Exciting because Fitch's Adam's apple is also tracing a line up and down his throat. Exciting because when his hand finishes its trip along my arm, it rests against my hand and I wiggle my fingers and he takes hold of them.

I have never felt anything as heavenly as Fitch holding my hand.

Until he steps even closer and his lips touch my cheek, then trail across it, to brush my lips.

I'm not sure if the tingles running through me mean I might faint, or I might explode.

I respond; pushing against him, and now there's no more brushing – our lips are fully pressed against each other's – and his are warm and soft, and then I feel his tongue, and even though this is where things stopped with Cade, this is not where it's ending – I'm not letting it end here – with Fitch. My mouth knows what to do, and so do my hands; they run up his sides – lean with muscle and slightly rippled over his ribs – then curl behind his shoulders and pull him tight to me; pull me close against him.

I sort of know his hands are on my waist and I'm kind of aware I'm between the wall of the cabin and his tall body, but mostly I just know there's nowhere else I'd rather be, and I can't get enough of him, and I want to snake my arms inside his shirt – not to touch his bare skin; or not *only* to touch his bare skin – but just to be closer to him; as close as I can get. I never want to stop touching him.

"Ahem!"

*What?*

There's a tap on my shoulder. "Sorry guys ..."

I pull back from Fitch and lean my head against the cheap cabin siding. My heart's hammering, lungs pushing against my rib cage. It's like I just ran a sprint, but better. There's no pain. I could keep going. And going, and going, and going ... and I would have if Miranda hadn't appeared out of the dark to pull me back to earth.

"Oh, I don't really want ice cream tonight ..."

Her furrowed brows lift, corners of her mouth curl up – her face blossoms into laughter for one, quick second – "Oh, Lace. As if I'd interrupt this –" She puts a hand on my shoulder and one on Fitch's. "– for ice cream."

"No." The seriousness falls across her features again.

"There's some major shit going down."

I look at Fitch, look at her. "What do you mean?"

"Come with me," she says. "I'll show you."

# Chapter Twenty-Two

---

We follow Miranda, our footsteps hollow on the plywood surface of the boardwalk.

As much as I wish I was still kissing Fitch, this is still OK, because he has his hands behind him, holding mine.

I'd walk pretty much anywhere like this.

Miranda's cabin is at the very far end of the boardwalk, and in contrast to the converted supply closet Carly and I share, I'm pretty sure Miranda's cabin must normally be a double classroom. Miranda's cabin always wins the housekeeping awards, and whenever I've been inside the tidy room, I've been impressed by the huge amount of space left in the middle, with all the bunks pushed tight against the wall.

Tonight all that space is filled.

Small bodies are everywhere. Little girls, heads together in groups of two or three. Some are talking, a couple are weaving friendship bracelets, but quite a few are sniffing, or wiping at their eyes, and a couple actually have tears streaming down their faces.

From what I can tell, most of the camp is crammed into this space, including the quiet counsellors we've never gotten to know very well. It's about five degrees warmer in here than on the porch, and the windows are steaming up.

There are three people missing. Ponytail, Juicy, and number three.

"What's going on?" I ask.

Miranda doesn't say anything; just leads us back outside and to the next cabin – the last one on the boardwalk. She points through the window. Inside are the three missing counsellors. The third one is lying curled up on her side on the floor. She appears to be sleeping. Juicy and Ponytail are sitting side-by-side, leaning against a bottom bunk, heads bowed over a cell phone.

"Do you have them *locked* in there?" Fitch asks.

"You betcha."

"You can't do that," he says.

"Too late; it's done." Miranda puts her hands on her hips. "They're drunk as skunks, and I told them they're not going anywhere until your mom gets here. She can decide what to do after that."

"My mom's coming?" Fitch asks at the exact same time as I ask, "Jan's coming?"

Just as I say her name, Jan appears out of the shadows with Carly by her side. "They're just up here," Carly's saying.

Jan's lips are tight. She looks at Fitch, and raises one eyebrow. Nods at me. Turns to Miranda. "You were the one who discovered this?"

Miranda nods.

"You come in with me, then," Jan says to Miranda.

Miranda pulls a key out of her pocket, opens the door, and they disappear inside leaving me and Carly and Fitch standing on the boardwalk.

"What happened?" I ask Carly.

She's quiet for a minute, and I wonder if she's going to answer me. Maybe I should have let Fitch ask her. But she takes a deep breath and starts. "I don't know everything, but Miranda said she was heading on the ice cream run ..."

Both Fitch's eyebrows go up, and I wonder if the mystery of the missing ice cream has been discussed in his household.

"... and she ran into two of the girls from Alanna's cabin on their way to the bathroom. They were crying."

I'm pretty sure Alanna is Ponytail.

"Why?" Fitch asks this time.

Carly points over her shoulder to the cabin Jan and Miranda are in. "Did Miranda tell you they're completely wasted? Apparently they've been meeting people they know – boyfriends or whatever – at the ski hill at night to party. Normally they must come back late, after the campers are asleep, but tonight, for some reason, they came back earlier, and the girls were awake and asked where they'd been, and they were so loaded, it got ugly."

Carly walks over to the window of the cabin with all the little girls inside. "The reason some of them are crying is I guess Patty threw up," – that's the girl asleep on the floor – "and Alanna told them to leave her alone, and that was upsetting enough for the kids, but Jessie," – the one I know as Juicy – "started telling all the kids exactly what she thought of them. Like 'you're fat,' and 'you have ugly clothes,' and 'you'll never have a boyfriend.'" Carly shakes her head. "What a mess."

Through the foggy window I can see one of the sensible, quiet, not-drunk counsellors scribbling on the whiteboard, conducting an impromptu game of Pictionary. All the faces in the room are turned to her, and even the kids who were crying look considerably more cheerful.

"Well," I say. "I guess we should get in there and help rally the troops."

"Yeah," Carly says. "I think you and I just became honorary counsellors."

It should be a bad night. I have a sliced-up arm, there are a bunch of traumatized kids in front of me, and I can't see any way there doesn't mean I have a lot of extra work ahead of me.

But Carly just said "you and I." My friend who's been really mad at me just put us together in the same sentence.

And Fitch – behind me I feel his hand placed flat on the small of my back, his pinky finger snaking just under my waistband, and I step back into his contact – well, Fitch kissed me.

He kissed me. This amazing, excellent, smart, gorgeous, funny, perfect-for-me guy kissed me.

So, on balance, I'm feeling OK about tonight.

Carly steps to the door, puts her hand on the knob.

"Carly?" I ask.

"Yeah?"

"Just one thing. What's the bucket in the corner for?"

She laughs. "A bunch of the kids were too shaken up to go out into the dark to go to the bathroom."

"Sorry you asked?" Fitch says.

"Sorry I asked."

I take a deep breath. "Let's go."

# Chapter Twenty-Three

I'm back in Jan's house. It's the first time I've been past the porch and this time I didn't have to weasel my way in with a creative excuse.

I'm sitting at a round kitchen table with Fitch on one side of me, and Miranda on the other. Carly's here too. For now the campers have been split into three groups, and put into the three largest cabins, each supervised by one of the remaining counsellors who isn't sitting at this table, and didn't get drunk on the ski hill tonight.

Owen has made hot chocolate, and we all have a mug in front of us. When he opens a bag of Decadent Chocolate Chip cookies my stomach gives a massive grumble. It's become accustomed to ice cream at this time of night. "Sorry!" I say, and grab a cookie.

I only have one hand free to dip my cookie and sip my drink, because Fitch is holding my other hand under the table.

I don't think his mom's noticed that he also only has one hand free, but Miranda has. She nudges me and whispers, "Nice."

I can't disagree. It's very, very nice.

Jan pours herself a cup of tea and sits down at the table with us, but with spaces on either side of her, so it's still clear she's chairing this gathering.

"So." She looks into her teacup, pinches the top of her nose, then looks up. "Well. That was a complete bloody mess."

I hiccup my hot chocolate, and Miranda snorts.

Fitch doesn't react, so I guess he's seen this slightly vulgar, quite unexpected streak of his mom's before.

Jan continues. "Obviously, I'm going to have to ask more of each of you. We're down three counsellors and camp is on-going. Even if I can hire anyone at this point in the summer, I can't imagine it will happen before the start of the next session, and I can't imagine finding three reliable people."

"Not that the original three were reliable," Miranda says.

Jan gives her a long look. "Quite."

"At any rate, this is what I'm proposing. The campers from the youngest cabin will be divided up and a few put into each of the other cabins – trying to keep friends together, and choose the most appropriate age groupings." Jan looks at Miranda. "This means you, and each of the other three counsellors will get about three new campers each for the remainder of the session."

I hold my breath. The next part affects me. I know it does because Jan is looking right at me. "The remaining two cabins will have to be covered by you two; Carly and Lacey."

"How on earth can Lacey do that? She's up at the crack of dawn, and she's at the barn until partway through the evening, and she's hardly back in-between." It's like Fitch is living in my head, articulating my concerns for me.

Jan's nodding. "I know. It's not ideal. But she can eat meals with her campers, and she'll sleep with them at night, and just spend as much time as possible with them."

I know it needs to be done. I don't see any other solution. But it means being *on* twenty-four seven. It means always having responsibilities. It also means there's no way I can go home for the rest of the summer. I have to run horseshows until after noon on the Saturday the campers leave and, if I'm a counsellor, I have to greet arriving campers as early as Sunday morning.

Carly clears her throat. "During the day, I can help keep track of Lacey's campers – make sure they get to the right activities."

I look at Carly. I've always liked her, but I also always thought she was a bit fluffy. I mean, she quit riding and started dating boys – that decision alone was hard enough for me to figure out. But we're sitting here, and I'm the one holding a boy's hand, and she's rolling her shoulders back and offering to work harder ... I speak up. "I can do my best. I'm not sure I'll be the best counsellor in the world, but I'll try."

"Thank you," Jan nods, and she's back to normal Jan. She pushes her chair back from the table and says, "You should probably all get some sleep now. The rest of this session is going to be very busy."

Owen clears away our hot chocolate mugs and the four of us walk to the door. Miranda and Carly toe their feet into their flip-flops and step out onto the porch, and I turn to Fitch. "Well, it was nice kissing you. It sounds like I'll basically never see you again now."

He laughs. "Hey, I'm not going anywhere." He leans forward and nibbles my earlobe. "I wish you could be my camp counsellor."

I've only ever read about people's knees going weak before, but now I know exactly how it feels. "Whoa."

There's a tinny rapping on the screen door. "La-cey ... we're go-ing ..."

"I've gotta go," I whisper.

He takes my hand and squeezes it. "It'll all be fine. You'll see."

◇◇◇

Miranda and Carly and I walk back three abreast.

You'd think we'd have a million things to say. You'd think we'd be spilling over with gossip, but I, for one, am too tired to even get the conversation going.

Despite the not-so-nice things that happened today, and the challenges we're going to face for the rest of this session – at least – I'm strangely relaxed walking through the inky summer night with these two. I like them both. The more I get to know them, the more I like them – fights over kissing boyfriends notwithstanding.

Miranda finally speaks. "So, Fitch."

Just hearing his name stretches a smile across my face. "Yeah, Fitch."

"Congrats," she says.

I sneak a look at Carly. I wonder if this is too much, too soon, too close to home. Even though I want to grab Miranda by the shoulders and jump up and down and yell, 'I know! Isn't he the best? Isn't it exciting?' I just say, "Thanks."

And I walk home to my last sleep as just a riding instructor.

# Chapter Twenty-Four

---

I had so much free time before.

Now I have to shower at what used to be ice cream time because, where the counsellors get time off when their kids are in activities, and I used to get time off when the kids were with their counsellors, now I'm responsible for both.

Miranda starts showing up in the pool shower room with two bowls of ice cream, and I sit on the narrow bench, littered with left-behind towels, and hoodies, and other little-girl belongings – my hair wrapped in a towel on top of my head – and I eat ice cream.

It's OK. It's doable. No camper gets completely neglected, but I always feel like I should be doing more. Too often when they want to paint my nails, braid my hair, I have to say, "I'm sorry. I have to go to the barn."

I feel like a great counsellor would be with them all the time. But I can't be.

Jan seeks me out the first day of my counselling duties to tell me about one girl – Stephanie – who was sent with warnings from her parents about anxiety.

"Anxiety?" I ask. "Like diagnosed or just nervous?"

"Diagnosed," Jan says. "She's been getting therapy at home

and they decided she was ready to try camp because she loves riding, and she could bring her horse, and her counselling had been going well ..."

I finish her sentence. "And then this happened ..."

Jan nods. "Yes. I can't imagine this will be good for her. Apparently it was one of the girls she's become close to who bore the brunt of Jessie's put-downs."

I take the opening. "What did happen with those three?" I ask. "What were they thinking?"

Jan sighs. "Well, according to two of them, I overreacted. I can't believe it, but their parents are backing them up. Saying our rules are too restrictive here, and it's no wonder the girls needed to act out."

She continues. "It's actually only Jessie who has apologized. Said she made some bad choices and bad mistakes. Wrote a letter, which her parents brought here. They're furious with her." She shakes her head. "Not that it really matters. I mean, there's no way I can let her off the hook, but it is at least *something* that she admits she was in the wrong."

I shake my head. A shudder runs through me at the thought of how my dad would react if I ever pulled anything like that. But maybe that's part of it; I'm lucky to have been raised with limits – knowing somebody was watching how I acted. Let's face it – I've grown up with a whole island watching how I act – if I misbehaved at noon, everybody would know about it by dinner.

Maybe I should feel sorry for those girls for not having that. And maybe one day I will, but not at midnight, when Stephanie's sobbing wakes me. I'm completely disoriented. My new bunk is a bottom one. It's on the wrong side of the room. It's too close to the door. *Where am I?*

I wake up enough to go to the girl's bunk. She's not quite awake. She's tossing and turning. When I touch her arm, she quiets. If I let go, she fusses again.

I crouch in the grainy grey dimness created by the night light one of the girls has plugged into the socket next to her bed, and the faint light washing in from the yard light outside. I want Stephanie to sleep. I want all the other girls to sleep. *I want to sleep.*

I sigh, drag my thin mattress onto the floor next to her bed, reach up and take hold of her dangling hand. This becomes the way we sleep through the nights.

⟨⟨⟩⟩

Fitch comes to lunch every day. Which would be better if we still sat at the same table. But, of course, I sit with my campers now. Still, he helps carry our food to the table, helps us clear away after. Half my campers have crushes on him.

If there's something really good, like fresh rolls, or cookies, he saves his and slips it to me on his way by our table.

Sometimes there are notes, too. I get to know, and love, his fast, spiky, slanting handwriting *Hey Tick-Tock. I miss my clock girl,* or *When are you going to ride, Join Up? I'll come and watch you.*

When I step out of the dining hall on the day of the second note, he's waiting for me by the door. "What's up with 'Join Up?'" I ask.

He rolls his eyes. "It's all my mom talks about; how you did this brilliant thing – this join up – to introduce the girls to riding. How it adds to the program. If I hear 'adds to the program,' one more time …"

"Are you saying you're sick of hearing about me?"

"Nearly, Join Up, nearly. If you were less cute the answer would be a definite yes."

"Six o'clock," I say.

"Six o'clock, what?"

"Six o'clock is when I ride now." I grin as he blinks. "Yup. In the morning." I shrug. "It's the only time I can."

"You must love that horse," Fitch says.

"He's got me. Hook, line, and sinker."

Fitch pushes my hair back from my face; tucks it behind my ear. It's nothing, really, but it sends a quiver through me. "Lucky horse," he says.

Ava comes around the corner. "Oh, hey La-cey. Hey Fitch," she sing-songs.

I straighten, wag my finger at Fitch. "You get to the pool and do some work Mr. Carmichael."

"And you get back to your campers, Miss Strickland."

Ava giggles. "I know you guys like each other."

I fall into step beside her. "Do not."

"Do too."

"Do not."

"Yes."

I laugh. "Maybe just a little."

"Oh!" She jumps beside me. Claps her hands together. "I'm telling Daniella! Daniella ..." and she's gone.

It's nice to like Fitch, and I'm glad he likes me, but at this rate we're going to spend about an hour together – total – by the end of the summer.

At six o'clock the next morning I'm already proven wrong, because as I settle onto Night's back, Fitch walks up to the ring and leans on the rails.

"Really?" I ask.

"Of course," he says. "Is it OK?"

"It's amazing."

He watches me warm up, then start leg yielding exercises between the quarter line and the rail.

After a while he says, "He definitely has a stiff side, doesn't he?"

I grunt. "You said it. This one."

"I think ..." He squints against the low-slanting rays of the rising sun. "... I think you need to move your inside leg further back."

I blow air up, moving a stray hair out of my eyes. "I kind of am."

"You're moving it back from the knee. Try moving your whole leg, from the hip."

*Do you think I'm an idiot?*

Thank goodness I don't say it, because next time, I make a conscious effort to move my leg back from my hip and – voila – Night nearly trips over himself side-stepping away from my now-very-effective leg. I actually have to slow him down and straighten him.

"Thanks," I say. "That was perfect."

"Thanks for not telling me to back off."

I grin. "It never crossed my mind."

But what does cross my mind is why a guy who's clearly so smart about riding, and has a whole stableful of horses at his fingertips, never rides, except for that one time when his mother had to twist his arm to make him hack with me.

⟨⊗⟩

I step out of the steamy shower to find Miranda with three bowls of ice cream. The third one is for Carly, who's also here.

"Oh, hi."

Things have been fine between Carly and me. But that's easy to say, because now that we don't share a cabin, we hardly see each other, and when we do, it's to hand groups of kids back and forth. Carly's much too classy to call me a boyfriend-stealer – or worse – in front of twelve and thirteen-year-olds.

For her to be here, it means ... well, I'm not sure what it means.

"I'm, uh, surprised to see you," I say.

"What kind of surprise?" she asks.

"Good?" I snug my towel tighter around my head, and try again, with authority. "Good."

Miranda clears her throat. "I'm just going to check ... *something* ... out there. *Somewhere*. Be back in a sec."

*Man,* she is so not subtle.

Carly exhales, through her nose, so I can hear it.

"Listen Lace, I know – I always knew – it wasn't your fault; the Cade thing. But it hurt my feelings. And, you know, when something hurts your feelings ..."

"I know," I say.

"Maybe it wasn't even exactly his fault, either. We weren't *officially* going out at the pork roast, but he knew I liked him. We'd ... well, the details don't matter, but it just changed everything hearing you guys had kissed."

*He* kissed *me*. It's so tempting to say it, but I think better of it. It can't really help.

Instead I say, "I should never have said anything because it was really nothing, Carly. Truly, nothing at all." A tiny part of me remembers I didn't feel that way at the time, but it's so easy to dismiss now.

She gives me a lopsided smile. "I know. I can kind of tell. I mean, you and Fitch are so ..."

"I'm sorry."

"No, it's nice. It's sweet. I didn't think of him as a nice guy, but he's really nice with you."

"Are you and Cade ...?"

She shrugs. "I don't know, exactly. I guess maybe we'll see on the next session break. Or, at least I thought we'd see on the next session break, but now we don't get much of a session break anymore, which is also part of the reason I came tonight."

"What do you mean?"

"Money."

Miranda slips back in. "Everything good here?"

"All good," Carly says. "I'm just getting around to telling Lacey about the pay thing."

"Hmmm ... yes." Miranda picks up her now very soupy ice cream. "I'll be interested to hear what she says."

"What?" I yawn as I unwrap my hair and towel it dry. It's been a long day. It's been a long series of days. I have to get as much sleep as I can lying on the floor next to Stephanie, and then get up with the rising sun.

The clean yoga pants and t-shirt I've changed into are soft and comfy.

I want to turn my brain off and finish my ice cream and lie down so I can think about Fitch.

Carly starts. "I went to see Jan after dinner, to ask about my pay – our pay – now that we're doing two jobs instead of one, and we don't get any more downtime, and we can't go home between sessions."

She continues. "You know what it's like – my parents are in the same situation as yours – it's always a challenge to balance the books on the farm, and ... well I'm not doing this job for fun, and the extra money would mean ..."

I chime in, "Actually being able to finish our first year at university. Maybe being able to go back for a second year. Oh, I know; I've done the mental math."

"Yeah, well, you might need to keep the extra money in your head, because Jan doesn't intend to pay us more."

I'm fully awake now. "Pardon? What are you talking about?

How can she not? We're doing the extra work." I'd just assumed the next installment of my pay would be higher, to reflect the fact that I'm now a riding instructor and counsellor. I'd figured I might get away with not having to find a part-time job at university – at least not for this year. Every time I've been tired, or felt pulled in six directions, I've thought, *You're here for a reason. It's all worth it. Keep your eyes on the prize.*

Now Carly's telling me there is no prize?

"Nuh-uh," I say. "That's not right."

"You're telling me. But she said something about cash flow, and having to pay those three for the rest of the session, and then she tried to say we're not actually doing two jobs – we're here anyway, so it's more like a few extra duties on top of what we already agreed, and there was a lot of 'we all have to pull together in situations like this,' and 'you'll get a great reference – I'll make sure of it,' and 'it's for the good of the girls.'"

"What did you say?"

"I didn't know what to say. I was pretty stunned. I knew it wasn't right, but I decided it was better to talk to you first – for us to work together – so, I'm here ..."

*Shit.* Even though I sometimes cause confrontations, I never really mean to, and I certainly don't enjoy them, but it seems like I've got a big one looming ahead of me. This isn't fair to Carly, and it isn't fair to me, and I'm going to have to deal with it. *Shit.*

"OK," I say.

"OK, what?" Carly asks.

"OK, I'll talk to her."

"When? You have literally no free time."

Miranda speaks up. "Tomorrow after lunch. Carly and I can team up and, between the two of us we can do an activity with our three cabins." She snaps her fingers. "We'll tie-dye t-shirts. It'll be fun. We'll even do an extra one for Lacey. We'll make it green for the money she's going to convince Jan to pay you."

"Thanks Miranda," I say, but she shakes her head.

"Don't thank me. I'd way rather be looking after a dozen extra kids than going to talk to Jan Carmichael about money."

I would too. But it's not like I have a choice.

# Chapter Twenty-Five

I'm glad I'm busy, because it's only when I have two seconds to think that my stomach starts churning.

When I'm riding Night, or bringing in the herd, or helping one of my campers mop up the orange juice she spilled, or teaching riding, my mind is on what I'm doing – what I have to do to get through the next five minutes.

When I have a chance to breathe, that's when I start thinking about talking to Jan. Talking about money. Talk about stressful.

Fitch is waiting for me at the barn when my last morning lesson is over. He walks to the dining hall with me. "I have to go into town with my dad now and help him load some supplies into the truck. I didn't want you to wonder why I wasn't around for lunch."

"Your dad's lucky to get to hang out with you."

"Yeah, well, I wish it was you and me going into town for lunch ... speaking of which, I know it's still a while away, but at session break, after the horse show on Saturday, will you come out with me?"

"Out?"

He stops, steps in front of me, takes my hands. "Yup. Out.

There are a million things I want to do with you. I figure we can at least get started with five or six of them."

I laugh. "Like what?"

"Say you'll come along with me and I'll start planning."

"Of course. Yes. I want to. The only thing is, Meg and Jared might drive up, since I can't go home. They might take me out for lunch. But you could come, too, and then you and I could do whatever we want after."

"Meg and Jared?" His brow wrinkles.

It's so weird that I have this new life – this Fitch life – and Meg and Jared know nothing about it. Nothing about him. I guess that might all change very soon. "Yeah. Jared's my cousin and Meg's his girlfriend – she's my best friend." I snap my fingers. "I tried to introduce you to them at the last session break. They came to pick me up. But they showed up and I turned around and you were gone, and then after that ..." After that I think of what a jerk he was to me.

"Pretty girl ..." He says the words slowly. His cheeks are pink.

"What?"

"That's what he called you: 'pretty girl.' And you hugged him, and he hugged you, and I thought ..." He shakes his head. "I was super-jealous."

I clap my hand over my chest. *Seriously? Jared?* "Sorry, did you say you were *stupid*-jealous?"

He laughs. "You nailed it. Stupid jealous. That was me. I fumed all weekend. I was mad at you for having a boyfriend and not telling me and making me like you. I was mad at me for liking you. I was mad at him for getting to call you pretty girl and getting to hug you."

"Wow, I would never have pegged you for the insecure type."

"I never have been, before."

"So what snapped you out of it?"

"If you could have seen yourself, dripping wet, telling me off in the front porch, well ..."

"I was so adorable, you couldn't resist me?"

"No – you looked so ridiculous I figured nobody else could like you, so you probably didn't have a boyfriend after all."

"You!" I punch him, and he grabs my hand and twists it behind my back.

"Let me go!" I say.

"Make me want to."

"How?"

"You're smart – figure it out."

I think for a minute. "OK. Fine. I was jealous too."

"Really?" His grip loosens, but the second I wriggle he tightens it. "When were you jealous?"

"In the dining hall. When you were – you know *not speaking* to me – and that ..." I hesitate, decide against saying "skank" "... that *girl*, sidled up to you and whispered in your ear."

His laugh is so sharp and fast, the breath driving it lifts my hair. "I was staring at you the whole time."

"Because you hated me and liked her ... at least that's what I thought."

"Sorry, what did you call it earlier?" he asks. "Stupid-jealous?"

I stop fighting his grip; lean back against him. "Yeah, well, it's a good thing we've both stopped being stupid."

As soon as I relax, he does too. He wraps his arms around me and whispers in my ear. "So, Saturday – apart from a possible interruption from Meg and Jared – you're mine?"

There go my knees again – a little sweet talk, and warm breath in my ear, and I'm putty in Fitch's hands. I swallow hard. "Yup. Saturday."

He kisses my cheek and lets go of my hand at the same time. "Gotta go! Dad's waiting!"

I watch him sprint away and I turn to go into the dining hall.

It's probably just as well he's not going to be around. It'll be better if the coast is clear when I go to the house to talk to Jan.

◇◇◇

"Good luck," Carly and Miranda both tell me when I hand my campers over to them.

I know Miranda's offering moral support, but Carly really means it – she needs me to have good luck because whatever I work out with Jan will affect her, too.

"Fingers crossed!" I hold my hands up to show my fingers and set off down the drive.

I've thought about this. I thought about it in the minutes it took me to fall asleep on the cabin floor last night. I thought about it while I groomed Night before and after my ride on him.

It didn't take me long to decide what to ask for, but I've spent time since going back and forth over the pros and cons. I think what I've figured out will work for everyone. I think it's a win-win-win, but whether Jan will think so ... well, there's only one way to find out.

I march up the stairs. *Don't hesitate. Back straight. Be cool.*

I rap my knuckles on the door. *Knock-knock-knock.*

I don't wait long before knocking again. I'm determined right now, and I can't let myself be sidetracked.

After the second knock, Jan comes to the door. She opens it, "Yes, Lacey?"

I inhale sharply through my nostrils. "May I come in, please?"

She lifts her eyebrows. "Is it important?"

"Yes, actually. It is."

She leads me into a room I haven't been in before. It's not big, but it's organized, so doesn't feel small. The desk faces into the room, so when she sits behind it, there's a chair for me in front of it. Jan looks at her watch. "Shouldn't you be ...?"

"Yes. I should be with my campers. That's part of what I'm here to talk to you about." I sit so straight in the chair, my spine doesn't touch the back. "Miranda and Carly are watching them right now, but I will have to get back, and that's because I'm doing two jobs, and I need to understand what my compensation will be for the extra work I'm doing."

Jan sighs. Pushes a paper out of her way. "I'm assuming you've been talking to Carly."

I shift from one seatbone to another. "It doesn't really matter if I've spoken to Carly. It's important for me to know."

"Well, if you've spoken to her – which I'm assuming you have – you'll know I explained to her that we just don't have the cash flow to increase your pay right now. It's very expensive running a business like this. The margins are razor-thin. We'd like to pay all our staff more, but it's simply not possible."

*Breathe. Don't lose it.* It's hard not to, because she's definitely talking to me like I'm stupid, but I know it won't help.

The anger rising in me might be OK, but only if I can harness it. What did I rehearse? What were the main points? I breathe deeply, and tick my fingers off against the outside of my thigh – down where Jan can't see them.

"Well, you see, that's exactly why I'm here. Both Carly and I really do understand small businesses. We've grown up on family farms where a razor-thin margin looks great. Carly and I are both working to pay our own way to university, and we're not asking for a raise; we're asking for fair pay to reflect the fact that we're doing a considerable amount more work than we originally were hired to do. Work you would have to hire additional staff members to do if we weren't stepping up."

This is where Jan would normally make a dismissive comment and leave the room and I'd be left wondering what to do next. If she does that now, I don't know what I'll do.

She purses her lips. "I wonder if we can make a deal?"

"It depends what the deal is." I'm trying not to let my voice shake, but all the rest of me is, so it's a tough fight.

"I need as many paying campers as I can possibly get. I know, for a fact, of two campers who booked for this session after taking the first session's riding lessons from you. I'm prepared to pay you half their camp fees as a sort of referral bonus on the grounds that they wouldn't have come back at all if it wasn't for you."

She sits back, folds her hands. "Bring me more new campers, I'll pay you more. Same offer for Carly, of course."

It's more than I expected. The fees here are steep. If Jan pays me that much, it's very close to what I would have said she owes me.

The temptation is huge to say, "Yes, please. Sounds great!" and run.

But while that would be me taken care of, it would only be me. Carly doesn't have the same leverage as I do. It's much easier to make an impression on kids when you teach them to pilot a horse. While they love sparkles and glitter glue, their parents aren't going to fork out huge sums of money for them to come back for an extra session just for that.

Carly does a good job, and she works hard. And she's my friend.

"Well ..." I say. "I appreciate the offer. I think we're getting somewhere."

"But?" I swear there's a smile tugging at the corners of Jan's mouth. If she wants to think this is funny, fine. I don't care, as long as I get a better deal for Carly and me.

"I have a counter-proposal."

"Which is what?"

"Since you feel able to pay that amount, you pay it to Carly."

"And what about you?"

I look her straight in the eye and cross the fingers on both my hands. "You give me Night."

# Chapter Twenty-Six

When I go back to retrieve my campers from Carly and Miranda, they turn to me with wide eyes and both ask, "Well?"

"Well, I think we're making progress."

"What did she say?" Carly asks.

"She said she'd think about it."

It's not the answer I wanted to give. I wanted to run back to Carly and say, "You're getting paid!"

As much as we seem to have put the Cade thing behind us, I wanted to seal the deal as best-friend-ever, by flashing a fistful of cash in front of her.

It kills me when she lays her hand on my arm. "Thanks for trying. I'm really impressed you had the nerve after she said no to me," and Miranda nods and says, "Yeah. She scares me."

Jan hasn't said yes, and she hasn't said no. The not-saying-no is what I should focus on. But I won't feel right until she says yes.

◈◈◈

"She should say 'yes,' shouldn't she?" I'm leaning over the gate of Night's paddock, giving him a final pat and carrot, before heading back to the cabin to spend what's left of the evening with my campers.

The light's gone hazy and dim. It's hot, and the campers all have deep tanlines, and lots of mosquito bites, and sun streaks burned into their hair, but the days are shortening.

Before I know it, summer will be over, and it'll be time to go to university and how much of it will I be able to pay for? And am I just being silly? Self-indulgent? Should I just be doing what my mom wants, and keeping my costs down by going to school at home?

Instead I've asked for another horse. Not something to make me money; something to cost me money.

"Except you'll be worth something, won't you? I can tell." I smooth Night's still-long forelock down the middle of his face.

"But the point is, you were worth nothing when I started riding you, and Jan got you for nothing, so I think it's a fair deal. I haven't asked her for money. I've just asked for you."

Night blows warm air into my face, and I blow back.

"You'd like to come live with Salem, wouldn't you? For a while, anyway. Until I have to sell you. But at least if you're mine I can choose who buys you. I won't sell you to somebody who's going to abandon you at a summer camp."

The gelding lifts his head and rests his chin on the top of my head. I giggle and reach up to scratch the bones of his face. "You are the only guy I would ever let get away with this," I tell him. "Even Fitch has to hold his own head up."

"Speaking of Fitch, time for me to go try to fit in a shower so the next time I see him I only smell a little bit like horse."

My riders have been talking about join up all session. I took them on a hack, and they liked it, but the join up talk hasn't stopped.

Finally, I ask, "Would any of you like to try joining up with your horses?"

In each group a few hands fly up. They're mostly the hands I expect – the hands of the most confident girls, who always want to try the next thing, and the next, and the next. There are also a couple I wouldn't have guessed at, and they're the ones I'd really like to try it with.

"So how about the rest of you?" I ask the girls who didn't put their hands up. "Do you still want to watch, even if you don't do it yourselves?"

The consensus is, Yes. Definitely.

"OK," I say. "Tomorrow's join up day, then."

⟨⟨⟩⟩

"Seriously?" I tell Fitch. "I can't believe I said I'd do this with them.

He's come to the pool house for the post-shower ice cream meet up, with his iPad in tow like I asked him to at lunch. "Can you connect to the staff WiFi from here?" I ask.

"Why?"

"I need to watch some videos. I've done join up with a beginner horse before, but never with a beginner rider. I'm hoping there's something on YouTube that'll help me."

"Which horses are you going to use?" Fitch asks.

"Good question. What do you think?"

And we're off. Discussing the horses least likely to stop dead and refuse to move. The ones that can be trusted not to kick a beginner who invades their personal space.

Miranda fakes a yawn. "Pardon me, but this is the dullest

conversation I've ever listened to," she says. "Carly and I are going to eat our ice cream outside."

I'm glad they're gone. It means I can sit on the sagging couch with my legs sprawled over Fitch's, watching join up videos. It means, when he says, "I've been making plans for the weekend," I can giggle and say, "Can't wait," and Miranda and Carly don't have to mime throwing up by sticking their fingers down their throats.

Finally there's a rapping on the door. "Lacey, we should really get back."

"'Kay," I say. "Be right there."

"You ready?" Fitch asks.

"As ready as I'm going to get before tomorrow morning."

"Good luck."

The heat's been stoking up again over the past few days, and there's sweat trickling down my temples as I stand just behind Ava. "Remember, Ava, stay behind him. When you step in front, you're telling him to stop. Right now you want to keep him moving."

We're working with Jeeves, a good-natured paint pony, who's loving the freedom of being loose in half the ring wearing no tack and no rider. His bucking and farting have drawn giggles from the watching riders, but he's settling down now.

"What do you see?" I ask.

"Licking and chewing," Ava says. It's what I've told them all to watch for. In fact, there are some murmurs from the girls leaning on the fence. "Licking and chewing ..."

"Good, so keep him moving, but relax a bit. You don't have to be chasing him."

"There ..." Ava breathes.

"What?"

"He dropped his head."

"Yes he did. Great. Just a little longer."

My fear is that one of these join ups isn't going to work. My fear is of a girl in tears when her pony won't walk over to her. I know all the girls are impatient so I'm working hard at maintaining my own patience.

*In three. In two. In one.*

"OK," I say. "You're ready."

I've been right beside her the whole time. Putting my hand on her shoulder to guide her position when I need to. Now I step away, and as I do, I tell her to do the same thing.

"You can walk away now."

I watch that moment – that gift – the lighting of her face. The delight, joy, trust that spreads through her features as Jeeves wanders over to her, as naturally as if there was never any doubt, and waits for her to acknowledge him.

"Go on," I say, "Give him a rub. Tell him he's good ... now go for a walk and let him follow you."

He does, as horses do once they've joined up, and Ava is already different. More confident. More sure of herself. In a way, more vulnerable, but it's vulnerability with power. She knows what it's like to wait, and hold your breath, and wonder if you'll be accepted. And she has been. So she'll be kinder to others, and more sure of herself.

At least, I hope she will be.

My stomach rumbles and I click back to the here and now, where I'm hot and hungry in the sand ring. Ava and Jeeves were my last pair of the morning. Next stop, lunch.

We did three join ups during the hour that just passed. The other two horses we used are being grazed by a couple of the girls on the lush grass that always grows around the fenceposts of sand rings – horse nirvana. "OK, girls. Pair up with the grooming, and you should be the first ones at the dining hall."

I'm following Ava out of the ring when I hear my name. "Lacey."

I turn to see Jan at the corner of the sand ring. What does she want?

If she's come to tell me off for working with the girls on join up, instead of riding, she can take a short walk off a long pier, as my dad would say. My core temperature is way too high, and my actual core – my stomach – is way too empty for me to be patient anymore.

And I'm tired. Just plain overall tired, from the long hours, and endless responsibility, and no breaks, and she should be afraid of me, not the other way around, because if I walk away, she is *screwed*.

I stride over to her with my shoulders back, chin jutted forward, and I wait for her to say something that will make me angry.

"That was very, very good."

"Oh." I'm almost disappointed. There's nowhere for all my stored up adrenaline to go.

"In fact, it's perfect timing. I got an email from one of the Toronto papers this morning. They have a running feature on camps within two hours of the city. They're considering sending a reporter, but they want to know what our angle is. There are dozens of riding camps out there – what makes us different?"

*I bet the rest of the camps pay their staff.* I bite my tongue, and wait.

"This ..." She gestures to the partitioned-off sand ring. "Is different. If I write back to them about this work you're doing with the girls, will you do a demo at the show day on Saturday?"

I think of Jan needing more campers who will pay more

fees, and I think of Carly and me wanting to get paid more. The old expression floats into my head. 'You scratch my back, I'll scratch yours.'

"Sure, I mean ..." I'm about to say I'll need the right set-up, and does she want me to do it with one of the girls, or just me and Night? And I'm not sure how it'll work if there are lots of people around, but before I can say any of that, she does her classic, "Great. Thank you Lacey," and walks away.

I can't easily follow her, because I'm behind a fence, and I'm not about to yell, so I just shrug. "Whatever."

I guess, like with so many things this summer, I'm going to have to wing it.

# Chapter Twenty-Seven

It's not really the physical exertion that's tiring me out, or even the lack of sleep – at least, I don't think it is – it's all the stuff in my head. Like:

- What's going on with Jan? I haven't heard from her. It's like our little chat – the one that took so much courage on my part to initiate – never happened. Do I have to confront her again? Should I be considering not coming back after this session? Do I need to call my dad about this?

- If I do leave, what about money? I was never going to make much working here, but if I leave before the final session, I'll make even less.

- School. Assuming I can go, and I have enough to pay for the first half of the year, how hard will it be to find a part-time job once I'm there? And will I have time to work and study?

- Speaking of school ... Fitch. What happens to us if the rest of the summer we hardly have time to see each other and then we leave for university? What's the point of figuring out we like each other if that's all we ever do? I'll be sitting in my rocking chair when I'm eighty saying, "There was this boy who liked me once, and I liked him ..." and my grandchildren will ask, "What happened?" and I'll say, "Nothing. We never actually spent any time together." Obviously the grandchildren in question would not be mine and Fitch's descendants.

Even though I say it's not the lack of sleep tiring me out, I'm happy to the point of giddiness when Stephanie hangs behind the other girls already plonking down on the dining hall floor for tonight's movie night, and tells me, "I think I can sleep through on my own tonight. I'm feeling much better."

I'm now thinking of the thin-mattress-on-springy-bunk set-up that seemed like an instrument of torture at the beginning of the summer, as a luxurious dream. I keep my smile in check – or try to – and say, "That's great news Stephanie. You can let me know if you change your mind."

Carly ushers her group in; guiding them to the front next to mine, then weaves her way through legs – crossed and sprawling – to stand next to me.

She's grinning so every dimple shows on her very cute face. I'd forgotten how adorable – how charming – Carly is when she's happy, happy, happy.

"What's with the big smile?" I ask.

"You know!"

"I wish I did."

"Oh, come on Lace ... we're getting paid!" She grabs my arm and does a little hop and a jump. "I don't know what you said, or how you did it, but Jan came over to the cabin after dinner and pulled me out for a minute." Carly's eyes widen now. "And you know what she's like – all scary and intense – and I thought my heart was just going to beat its way free; slip right between my ribs ... but she said I was going to get paid for all the extra work and I. Cannot. Believe. You. Pulled. It. Off!"

Carly grabs Miranda who's just brought her group into the dining hall. "Did you hear what Lacey Strickland Miracle Worker did? Double ice cream for this girl tonight, with whipped cream and chocolate syrup."

"You're getting paid?" Miranda asks.

Carly nods. "Yup. Getting paid!"

I'm really, really glad Carly's getting paid. It's amazing news. But ... where does that leave me?

I guess, worst case scenario, I'll just have to ask Carly for a loan halfway through the school year.

I'll say one thing for working pretty much non-stop – the session has flown by.

If I thought the end of last session was intense with all the bathing, and braiding and horseshow prep I was immersed in, this session I go through all that at the barn, then come back to my cabin to find what looks like a suitcase explosion in the middle of the room.

Girls trading t-shirts, and bracelets – "So, I'll always remember you." Girls shoving clothes into nooks and crannies that don't really exist in their bags. Stephanie saying, "Whoops!"

"What is it, Steph?" I ask.

"I packed everything."

"Good for you."

"No, like *everything*. My breeches, my show shirt. Even my underwear for tomorrow."

"Oh."

"And that stuff's all at the bottom of my bag."

"Double oh." I sigh; drop to my knees. "Here, I'll help you dig."

Why do I feel like nobody's going to get much sleep tonight?

This is not my first rodeo.

Or horseshow – whatever – but it's ridiculous how everything feels simple, straightforward, easy, even though I've really only done this once before.

I'm ready for the girls' nerves. I'm ready for their parents' nerves.

And the nicest part is, while it's easy to gloss over those parts of the show, I'm still just as proud of all my riders. Just as buoyed up by their smiles. Just as happy as they are when they attach their ribbons to the buttonholes of their jackets and puff their chests out.

"Good job!" I say it a hundred times. "Your daughter was a pleasure to teach." I say that eighteen times, and today add, "Your daughter was a pleasure to have in my cabin," a dozen more times.

Stephanie's parents take me aside. "Stephanie always has a hard time with homesickness. When we heard what happened with her counsellor, we were afraid that would be it – there was no way she'd stay. But you gave her support and she had a great time, and she's actually asking for us to let her stay for the next session."

Jan will be happy. Another new camper – with a new set of fees – to add to my tally.

It's only when Jan announces the end of the novice section of the show over the loudspeaker that I have a frisson of nervousness. I know what's coming next.

"Before we move onto the intermediate students," she says. "I'd like to take a few minutes to tell you about something special we've had added to our novice program this year. We were very lucky to hire Lacey Strickland as an instructor, and Lacey brings with her a fresh approach to horsemanship. If you'll look at the pen to the side of the ring, you'll see what I mean.

Owen and Fitch spent yesterday moving temporary fencing

into place to form a round pen.

Bonus: it's the first time I've had an actual round pen to work in.

Downside: there are dozens of gawping parents, and fidgeting siblings, and ponies milling about snatching at grass, and I've got no idea if Night is going to pay any attention to me at all.

My bad. I should have had more faith in him.

Even with all the movement and distractions, even with Jan's voice ringing out every now and then to explain what I'm doing – "You'll see the horse's ear is now flicking toward Lacey. She's watching for signs like this from him," – Night is laser-focused on me. Maybe even more than usual. I guess I'm the only thing he trusts in this busy place, and he's not going to let his attention wander from me.

Once I see it's going to go fine – he's going to give a great join up demo to our audience – I'm able to enjoy the slide of his muscles under his thin, glossy coat. I love how he carries his tail, and admire how his still-wild mane and tail save him from being too pretty.

It stops being a performance and starts being an honest-to-goodness bonding session. *Follow me here.* He does. *Trot after me.* He does that too. I'm pulled out of my Night zone by clapping. It starts with Ava and spreads through a gaggle of my riders, all lined up along the temporary fencing.

I stop in my tracks, feel a flush spreading through my cheeks, and give a making-fun-of-myself bow. Night stops with me and flings his head up and down, twice. I know there's a fly buzzing around his ears, but the watching parents don't. They laugh and clap, too.

Well. *Phew.* That went better than expected.

Fitch meets me at the gate. "Nice work Join Up."

"I never know what nickname you're going to pull out."

"Well, that clearly wasn't a Tick-Tock performance but I

don't want to over-inflate your ego by calling you 'Rock Star.'"

"Oh, by all means, whatever you do, don't inflate my ego."

He hooks his arm around my neck and pulls me in to kiss my forehead. "I like your ego just the way it is."

I look up and Jan is watching us.

*Ah-ha.* So I guess she knows I like her son.

Which is just one more thing she knows about me, while I still don't know what's in her head.

⟨⟨⟩⟩

I'm done. My riders' mounts are turned out. The cabin's empty – I'll sleep here alone tonight – and I'm off the clock. For less than twenty-four hours but, still, off the clock.

This time when Jared and Meg arrive, Fitch and I are sitting side-by-side on the stairs in front of my cabin waiting for them together.

This time when I jump up to greet them, I hug Meg first, then turn immediately to Fitch. "Fitch, I'd like you to meet my cousin, Jared and my best friend, Meg."

Meg is perfect – "Hi Fitch. It's really nice to meet you," – she's friendly enough to show, 'Yeah, I've heard of you,' but not embarrassing like, 'You're all Lacey ever talks about.'

Which, considering I only told her about him a few days ago, when she confirmed she and Jared would be here to take me out for lunch, is true – I haven't been talking about him all the time. Although, sitting in the truck, looking at the backs of the sun-tanned necks of my two favourite guys in the world – not including my dad – with Meg holding her hand in front of her lips and mouthing to me, 'He is so *cute!*' I'm tempted to make up for lost time by telling her just how cute Fitch really is.

When we get to the diner, the burger I order not only lives

up to my memory, but actually tastes better than I remember it.

"So, you swim Fitch?" Meg's eyes are wide with polite interest.

"Yeah. I love it. Technique is really important in swimming and it uses almost all of your body. Working at swimming – trying to understand the biomechanics of it – is part of what made me want to study Kinesiology."

"I hear that's a great program," Meg says. "Where are you going?"

"Wilfrid Laurier."

Meg kicks me under the table. Hard. I might need a kinesiologist to look at my leg after her blow. "Hmm ... that's really close to Guelph, isn't it? Where Lacey's going?"

*Is it?* I mean I kind of know it's not far, but the geography of Southern Ontario is a bit of a mish-mash to me.

"Thirty-five minutes away," Fitch says right away. Then, for the first time, I get to see how he blushes. It starts with two blooms of red, high on his cheeks, and spreads across his cheekbones to disappear into his hairline. "I mean, about half-an-hour. I think."

He puts down his burger, holds up his hands, and grins. "It's not like I plugged it into Google maps to find out how close I'd be to Lacey. I don't like her *that* much."

He winks at me, and mouths, 'Yes, I do.'

I'm stunned into silence. Fitch has thought about how we'll see each other during the school year. Fitch is planning ahead. I knew he liked me, but he's so smart, and funny, and drop-dead smoking-hot gorgeous, I always figured I was the lucky one – now I know for sure he likes me just as much as I like him.

It feels better than my burger tastes to just sit and think about that for a while.

*Wow.*

"Well, that might be good," Meg says.

"Why?" I ask.

"You tell 'em Jared. I've hardly eaten anything."

Jared pushes his now-empty plate to the side. "Well, the thing is, Meg and I were wondering if you could come back some weekends in the fall, Lacey. I was afraid it might be too far, but if you two could drive together – we could use your help, too ..." He looks at Fitch.

"Help for what, Jared?" Either my mind's still stuck in ga-ga land over Fitch, or Jared's not explaining himself at all.

"Oh. Yeah. Sorry. Well ..." He looks at Meg, and a more toned-down version of the blush I just saw on Fitch's face, spreads across Jared's. I suck my breath in. For a minute I think he's going to tell me they're getting married and, for some reason I still haven't figured out, that means they need me to be home on weekends.

"... Meg and I are going into business together."

"Business?"

OK, so it's maybe not as romantic as I first thought, but Meg's eyes are sparkling, so obviously she's happy.

Meg nods and takes over the explanation again. "I talked Jared into planting a field with really cheap corn. It was low-yield – we didn't care – it just needs to grow tall and green."

"Oh-kay ... why?"

She grins. "Because we're going to run a corn maze."

"A corn maze?" This time Fitch is asking.

"Mm-hm." Meg sips her drink. "It's actually ridiculous how much people will pay to go through a corn maze and, since Jared owns the equipment and the land, the upfront costs were nearly nothing. We cut the maze ourselves – which took ages; you wouldn't believe how complicated it is – but it was kind of fun to do together. I mean, if we make as much as we think we will, maybe we'll pay someone else to cut it next year ... but, sorry, jumping ahead."

She shakes her head. "I'm just so excited. Anyway, the main thing we need is just people to help us out – staff – for the weekends when it'll be really busy, and our first choice would be you." She reaches her hand out to me. "And you, too, of course Fitch, if you like."

She looks at me. "I thought it would help you make some extra money for school, and give you a chance to be home. And you don't have to say yes – you can think about it – but I hope you'll come."

I laugh. "I'm pretty sure I'd love to." I turn to Fitch. "And I guess we can talk about whether you'd want to, too. But, seriously, Meg – this is a real money-maker?"

"I think so. I've been doing research. I think it's worth trying."

Jared cuts in. "You know, I wasn't sure at first, either but Meg showed me the numbers. It looks good." He sits back and leans against the back of the booth. "Like Meg says, it's definitely worth a try."

*Wow.* Meg keeps talking while I work through my fries. A job for me – and maybe one for Fitch – and money for the farm, and a partnership between Meg and Jared, all from cutting paths through a field of corn?

I don't know if it's crazy, but Meg's never let me down.

When I sit back in the booth, my shoulders straighten a little more easily. We might not all be set for life, but it seems like I might have less to worry about than I thought.

I'll take it.

# Chapter Twenty-Eight

When we get back to camp, the driveway is still narrowed with trailers being loaded to take horses back to various barns around the province, interspersed with family cars, overflowing with duffel bags, pillows, and excited girls.

"Just drop us off down at the road," I tell Jared. "We can walk from there."

Fitch and I don't hold hands as we weave our way through equine and human bodies, pick up towels and stuffies dropped from bags, and call, "Bye! Have a safe trip home!" But we walk close enough for all my senses to be concentrating on the side of my body nearest to him. Sometimes our hands swing and brush, and it's like an electric shock fizzing through me.

When we get to a bit of a clear space in front of his house, I turn to him. "So? What's next?"

"What do you want to be next?"

I shake my head. "Uh-uh. You're not putting this on me. You said you were making plans."

He looks at me for a long minute with those crazy clear eyes, and the breeze blowing that always-unruly lock of hair over them, and I'm so tempted to say, 'OK, forget it. I'm deciding after all. We're going to my empty cabin to make out.'

Just in time he says. "Swimming."

"As in swimming-hole swimming?"

"That very kind of swimming."

"Oh! Excellent! I'll get my suit and meet you in front of the cabins!"

⟨⊗⟩

When I come back out of my cabin, wearing my swimsuit under my shorts and t-shirt, with a towel slung over my shoulders, Fitch is already in front of the cabin, but he's not alone.

He's standing with his mother, facing a couple. The man is talking with lively hand gestures, and the woman is nodding.

I hesitate, but Fitch gestures to me. There's something tense about the motion – it has a 'get over here' quality to it, as opposed to a 'why don't you join us?'

My mouth goes dry and I swallow, hard, once.

It's probably nothing.

As I get closer, the man breaks off his monologue to Jan and turns to me with a wide grin splitting his face.

He has the kind of hair that's gone grey just the way you'd choose for it to go grey if you were a mature man. The arm he reaches out to me is lean and, when I shake his hand, I discover it's strong, too.

His casual clothes are made with the type of fabric and tailoring that tell me they cost more than the best suit – the *only* suit – my dad owns.

Dads like this aren't uncommon in the horse world, but by mostly riding with Meg, I haven't had many dealings with them. Until now. For the last six weeks I've been teaching their daughters. And I like them. The daughters, that is.

This man's daughter is sweet and quiet – an intermediate rider who I didn't teach in the ring, but was in my cabin – she's standing some distance away by a massive black Land Rover. When I wave at her, she smiles. For her sake, I say, "Hello. You must be Mr. Knapp. Nice to meet you."

"The pleasure is all mine. It was a treat to watch you work with that horse. And Brit told us, over lunch, she almost wished she could have taken novice lessons to be in your group."

I smile. "Well, that's nice of her, but I'm sure she would have missed the jumping."

"We were just explaining to Mrs. Carmichael here ..." I love how Jan gets the "Mrs." treatment; even from the richest of parents, "... that we've been looking for a new prospect for Brit ever since she outgrew her large pony at the end of last season."

I nod. *Uh-huh. Whatever.* Fitch is so, so close. He looks so, so good. I really want to go swimming with him.

"That's part of the reason we sent her here; we know the school horses are decent, so it would keep her in the saddle while we were searching." He claps his hands together and makes a brushing movement, "But, of course, we never knew we'd actually find the right horse here."

*Oh. Now wait a minute ...* prickles are running up the back of my neck.

"Yes, we just loved that horse you were working with. Mrs. Carmichael was telling us how far you've brought him in just a few weeks. He seems to have everything we'd want. Looks, smarts, and lots of potential." He gives me a wink. "Your boss here should be very happy with you. Not only have you sold us another session of camp – Brit's asked us to let her stay on – but you've also sold a horse."

I can't breathe. I really, really can't. The thumping of my heart is squeezing my lungs so the oxygen won't flow in.

*I can't lose him.*

It's not just the money, although Jan certainly owes me something and if it isn't this horse ... well, if it isn't this horse I don't want to think about what it is. There's nothing else I want. I love Night. I don't ever want to sell Night. And if I ever did sell him, it would never be to somebody who thinks a green horse, just a few weeks out of turn-out, is a suitable mount for their shy, intermediate daughter.

Fitch saves me.

Or at least that's what it feels like.

He's not rude, but he's strong. He's decades younger, and considerably less powerful than the man in front of us, but Fitch stands right up to him. With a smile, but a strong voice, he says, "I'm afraid my mother didn't get a chance to finish what she was about to say – did you Mom?"

Jan looks at him, looks at me, then faces Mr. Knapp again.

No matter how long I know her. No matter what she does in the future, I doubt I will ever like Fitch's mom as much as when she opens her mouth and says, "I'm very sorry for the confusion, Mr. Knapp, but the gelding in question – Night – actually belongs to Lacey. So, as you see, even if I wanted to, I'd be unable to sell him to you."

Brittany's mom speaks up for the first time. She lays a hand on her husband's arm while looking at me. "And, I'm guessing from what we saw earlier between you two, he's not a horse you'd consider selling – is that right?"

I nod, gasp for air, while trying to keep it from being obvious I'm gasping for air. "Yes. That's right. I'm afraid he's not for sale."

And now I really want them to go, because I think my knees are about to collapse.

The still waters of the secluded quarry are deep, cold, and clear enough to show all the rocks shelving away for metres and metres below the surface. I swim across, and back, and that feels like hard work, but Fitch does it twice in the time it takes me to do one crossing, and when I pull myself out, wetting the rocks at the edge of the water, he calls me a lightweight, and sets off again.

There's an expanse of flat, dark rocks between here and the path, and as I spread out on them they're hot under my wet skin. I also find they curve, ever-so-gently, away from me on all sides; pushing up under my spine, opening my chest and shoulders.

It's a warm, stretchy, heavenly feeling.

I use the time to myself to let my brain drift; to torture myself; replaying that moment where I thought Night was gone, safe in the knowledge that he's not, and never will be.

Unless we can't afford to keep him. I still have to tell my dad I'm bringing another horse home. *Worry about that later ...*

I roll my shoulders against the smooth, black rock. *Feels. So. Good.*

Until a massive shadow blocks out the sun. It could be a rain cloud because there are also water drops landing on me.

I open one eye. "Seriously Fitch? I was in paradise here ..."

He crouches but makes sure to keep his body between me and the sun. "And? You aren't still in paradise?"

"Not since this big hulking creature stole my rays."

"Wow. That sounds terrible. Who would do that?" He places a hand on either side of my head, and lifts his leg over me, so his knees are on either side of my hips. Then he stays like that and drips.

"Fitch! You are terrible!" I squirm, and twist, but he pulls his knees tighter so my hips are held in place.

"Tell me how terrible I am." His face is really, really close to mine. His breath is warm, and most of the water has already run off him.

On second thought, maybe this isn't the worst place to be.

"Awful," I whisper.

"You know what's awful?" he asks.

I gulp, and my gulp is louder than my question. "What?"

"I haven't kissed you in forever."

"That is ..." I don't get to finish my answer because his lips are on mine, and I'm lifting my head to meet him, and while he kisses me everything disappears – is fuzzed out – from my brain. There's no Carly, or Miranda. No twelve new campers arriving tomorrow. There's no farm, and no worries about it. There's even no Night. Not right now.

Right now, there are just my eyes, sneaking a look at our bodies; I've never loved my body so much as I love it now with my legs tangled with Fitch's; our hips and chests pressed together.

And there are the sounds that mean nobody's around – the singing of birds, sighing of the wind, trickling of water somewhere underwater – and our breathing; faster and heavier than normal. Like when I'm done working Night through a tough leg yield. Like when Fitch has just been swimming.

And Fitch's hard muscles just under his soft skin which, at first was cool to my touch, but warms when I spread my hands across his broad back; lowering them to where his waist tapers in a classic swimmer's shape.

He tastes great, too. "You taste like toothpaste," I giggle when I pull my lips off his for a second.

"So do you," he whispers it in my ear, and every muscle in my body reacts; back arching to push me against him, foot twining around his.

"Well, I knew you'd want to kiss me, so I brushed my teeth," I say.

"I like a girl who plans ahead."

I nibble his ear. "Oh yeah? Are there lots of girls who plan ahead for you to kiss them?"

"Not at the moment."

I lift my hand to smack at him, and he catches my wrist, lowers it back to the rock and kisses me again.

We kiss for a long time. We kiss until his face, which seemed smooth enough at the beginning, turns out to have just enough stubble on it to make my cheeks sore. We kiss until he works his way down my neck which nearly turns me inside out with a kind of ticklishness I've never felt before. Instead of wanting to push him away, I want to pull him closer, like that will ease the jolting currents jumping across my skin and through my nerves.

He works his way to the edge of my swimsuit top, then he pauses and, with the hem held between his teeth, his eyes find mine.

A thrill runs through me – of fear, excitement, and something else; something new to me. Arousal probably. Temptation. I want him to pull harder. I want that bathing suit slipped down.

It feels like the biggest decision ever.

Fitch makes it for us. He releases the stretchy fabric, and rocks forward again to kiss me on the cheek. "Probably shouldn't."

"Probably shouldn't *today* ..." I correct, then wink.

"Oh, geez, Lace. Don't wink like that. It's completely frigging adorable. You're going to kill my willpower."

I wriggle to a sitting position and pull my t-shirt over my head. "Speaking of adorable ..." I trace my finger across his untanned chest. "This fish-belly-white look is super hot. Since you spend half your life on an outdoor pool deck, it wouldn't kill you to catch a few rays."

He shrugs. "Nah ..." then points to a scar between his ribs. "This doesn't really tan, so ..."

"So, what?" I ask. I instinctively reach toward it, then pause; hovering my fingers over it. "May I?"

"Um, OK." His mouth might have told me to go ahead, but his body language says otherwise. He tenses and holds himself extremely upright while I press my fingers softly to the seam of thickened skin.

"There's nothing wrong with this, Fitch. It's part of you." I look at him; wait until he meets my eyes. "Can I ask what happened?"

He fixes his gaze on something in the distance. "Do you ever wonder why I don't ride? Or not much?"

I nod. "All the time. You're so smart. You know so much about it. You're so great when I'm riding Night."

"Well, I had an accident. Or, it wasn't exactly an accident. We had this nightmare pony – he was called Sandcastle – sounds sweet, but he was truly nasty. Anyway he ran me into the arena boards. Hard. On purpose. Right where one of the studs bumped out. I don't think he planned it that well – that was just by chance – but it cracked my ribs. And then my lung collapsed. And then ..." He shrugs. "Well, hospital, chest tube, scar, etc."

I shiver, thinking of the Fitch I at least really like, and could definitely imagine myself loving, being so badly hurt. It could have been so much worse. He could have died. And then I wouldn't be sitting here in the sun, feeling the distant thumping of his heartbeat through his ribs.

He continues. "It's not like I'm scared, exactly. I mean, I'm aware – obviously – of what can happen when you ride." His hand instinctively finds his scar, brushing my hand as it does. I take a light hold of his pinky. "The thing is, I never really loved riding. It wasn't in my DNA. But, you know, I didn't have a way out before. No excuse not to ride with all those horses in the barn, and my mom wanting me – *expecting* me, really – to be on a horse every single day. The accident gave me an out. Even my mother couldn't force me to ride after that happened."

"I'm sorry," I say.

"Don't be. I got to swim. Which, as it turns out, is in my DNA. So I'm glad it happened. It got me here."

I straighten, crawl around in front of him so I can be sure he's looking at me; not a craggy tree up the hill, not a passing cloud. "That's exactly it, Fitch. Salem, my horse at home, has tons of scars. Horses that get ridden and turned out, just do. Her scars – well some of them worried me when they happened – but when I brush her; when I see them, they remind me of the things we've been through together, and they show me she's *her*.

"And Night; I'll know he's really mine when I can find all his scars blindfolded."

Fitch grins. "He *is* really yours."

I give an exaggerated exhale. "Thank goodness for that. I nearly died back there. Thank you so much for sticking up for me."

He smiles. "I was ready to punch that guy if you needed me to."

I cross my hands over my chest. "You're the first guy who's ever offered to carry out an act of violence on my behalf. It's surprisingly touching."

Fitch stands, reaches his hand to pull me up. "Lacey Strickland, this is my official offer to mess anyone up, any time you like. Just ask."

I stand beside him, and lean in to whisper in his ear. "Seriously, though, thank you for showing me your scar."

"Do you have any?" he asks.

I wink again. "That's for you to find out."

# Chapter Twenty-Nine

---

I wake up at riding-Night-before-bringing-in-the-herd time. I wake up before the sun has even broken the horizon line. I wake up ridiculously early.

I don't mind, though.

Opening my eyes in the quiet cabin – empty of girls who may be adorable, but snore like sailors, and smell surprisingly bad at certain times – lets me appreciate the fact that I'm still here. In bed. Under the covers. Head on my pillow. Not moving. Not going anywhere at all.

Rolling over and going back to sleep.

Waking up half-an-hour later.

And going back to sleep.

Waking up again. Thinking about it for a few minutes. Pointing and flexing my toes. Stretching my arms over my head. Pointing my left hand, then my right one at the bunk above me. Finally giving a huge groan and just rolling, duvet and all, right out of bed and onto the floor.

There. I'm up. Or down. But out of bed.

None of the rest of the staff are here. They all said goodbye to their campers mid-morning yesterday and, unlike me, who had to stay for the horse show, had time to go home. The dining hall isn't opening to feed breakfast to me, so Fitch has invited me to eat at his house.

"Really?" I said.

"Well, yeah, of course. You kind of need to eat."

"I won't die. I have a couple of stale bagels and a brown banana stashed in the cabin."

"Don't be stupid, Lace. I'm going to show you how bacon and eggs should be cooked."

"Who says I don't already know?"

"Because you haven't eaten mine."

I didn't argue too hard because, of course, I wanted to have breakfast with Fitch. Although having breakfast with Jan could be creepy. Maybe she won't be there ...

I check the time. Half-an-hour before I'm supposed to be at Fitch's. Perfect. I can start my day with a hot shower – I never knew how much of a luxury that was when I was living at home – then fill my stomach with great food. The best breakfast, apparently, I've ever had. Fine with me.

◇◇◇

This time I don't have to stand, and stare at the door, and wonder how I'll get inside.

This time Fitch is waiting for me, looking bed-rumpled – in a good, mussed-hair, creases-on-cheeks way – smelling like bacon and eggs – delicious – and wearing an apron over his white t-shirt and surf shorts.

I giggle.

"What?" he asks.

I tug at the strap.

"You like?" he asks.

"Oh yeah, it's very manly."

"Are you questioning my manliness?" He steps toward me

and I step back, against the wall, and as I'm breathing in, he's pressing his lips to mine.

There's nothing soft, or teasing this time. He's insistent; kissing me hard and fast, sparking something in me I've only felt fleeting hints of before, so that I'm pushing forward against him, I'm running my hands up his back; digging my nails into his skin.

Kissing, kissing, kissing. Harder, never pausing, hardly breathing, fingers twined in each other's hair.

He snags a strand of my hair and I whimper.

"Lace ..." He pulls away, breathing hard.

"Sorry," I say. "Your mom. Is she ...?"

He swipes the back of his hand across his mouth. "Fund-raising pancake breakfast at the community hall."

"Oh, phew. That's good. But still ..."

He nods. "Yeah, still. We should probably actually eat breakfast."

"Fitch?" I say.

"Yeah?"

"You're manly."

We sit at the round wooden kitchen table, eating bacon, and eggs, and bagels, and drinking fresh-squeezed orange juice. I sweep my hand wide. "How did you ever think I could eat all this?"

"I thought you might want a doggie bag for later. Break-fast-for-dinner? You know – when you're back to dining hall food."

I groan. "Don't remind me. I'm still on vacation for a few more hours."

"So, what do you want to do with the rest of your vacation?"

"Mmm ..." I stretch, reach my hand into a ray of sun streaming through the kitchen window. "How about coffee by the pool?"

"You like coffee?" he asks.

I grin. "OK, fine, call my bluff. Hot chocolate. Coffee just sounded more sophisticated."

We're walking along the drive toward the pool house, talking and laughing and trying not to spill our steaming mugs of hot chocolate, when the sound of a car engine, cruising very slowly up from the road, makes me stop and turn around.

No. Way.

I shake my head. "Nuh-uh, Fitch. There *cannot* be a parent thinking of dropping a camper off this early. It's not fair, not acceptable, and not going to happen."

"I don't think it's a parent, Lace."

I look more closely. Fitch is right. It can't be a parent because the car is tiny; definitely without the needed trunk space for an overstuffed duffel bag, and a favourite pillow, and riding boots and a helmet.

So I'm off the hook.

Except ... I recognize that car. I'm not much for cars, but the sleek lines of this one say "money" even to me.

It's a Jaguar, I think. Sonny has a Jaguar convertible. A red Jaguar convertible.

I squint. Sonny has a profile that looks very much like the one turned sideways studying Fitch's house as the car rolls along.

And the woman next to him. It took me a few seconds with the scarf and dark glasses she's wearing, but it's my mom.

Oh. Wow.

What are they doing here?

I'm about to find out, because my mom's spotted me now, and she's tapping Sonny on the shoulder and pointing to me. He stops the car, and my mom waves her hand at us.

I walk over, feel like a giant standing next to the low-slung car. "Hey, wow! What are you guys doing here?"

My mother beams at me. "Well we so enjoyed having you over the last time you were home, and when you emailed to say you couldn't come this time, Sonny suggested we just come here instead."

"I'm ... amazed."

My mom reaches up to lay her hand on my arm. "Well Sonny found us the nicest inn at a winery – who knew there was a winery in this area? – so we had a lovely dinner last night, and a wine-tasting, and now here we are."

"That is ..."

Sonny's already out of the car, walking around, grabbing me in a hug. "Great! It's just great to see you Lacey. We just had coffee this morning – no breakfast – because we thought you might let us take you out."

"Well, the thing is, I ..."

"The thing is," I turn my head to see Fitch behind me. "The food here isn't that great, so Lacey loves a chance to eat out." He puts his hand out to Sonny. "I'm Fitch."

Sonny's smile widens as he takes Fitch's hand. He likes his directness, his confidence, his handshake.

My mom's grip tightens on my arm. She likes Fitch's drop-dead-dreamy good looks.

I guess I can't blame her.

"Nice to meet you, Fitch," Sonny's saying. "Would you like to join us for breakfast? You could probably guide us to the best place around."

"I'd love to, if I'm not in the way."

My mom's hand flutters at her breastbone. "Oh no, definitely not in the way. Please come along."

"We'll just take these mugs back to Fitch's and meet you in front of the house," I say.

As we walk back, I say, "We just ate!"

"Yeah? And?"

"Why didn't you let me tell them that? How can you think of eating again?"

Fitch sets his mug on the top step and reaches for mine. "Let me give you a little tip, Tick-Tock. When your parents want to spend money on you, you should always let them; it makes them feel good. And when you're offered good food, you should always say yes."

"That was two tips," I say.

"Well, the second one's free, just 'cause I like you so much. Now, come on, you should see the breakfast they serve at the diner."

◇◇◇

Fitch is right. The breakfast at the diner is worth having as a second complete meal.

I take a sip of pulpy sweet orange juice. "Fitch, you were right. This is the best breakfast I've ever had."

Fitch raises his eyebrows. "Really?"

I nod. "Mmm-hmm. Definitely. Never tasted bacon cooked so perfectly."

"Never?"

"Never, ever."

"I give you this is good, Lacey, but I'm sure you've recently had a breakfast that was just a little bit better than this, haven't you? Think about it."

"Mmm ... yeah ..." I take a bite of bacon. Chew. Swallow. "No, nothing's coming to mind."

He puts his foot on top of mine under the table, and I put my other foot on top of his.

Fitch makes everything fun, and I'm not the only one who likes him.

He asks questions about Sonny's business, and he listens to my mom's tales of singing in coffee houses in New York. It was decades ago, but you'd never know it from the way she tells the stories.

When Sonny asks him about school, Fitch answers directly.

When the bill comes, Fitch pulls out his wallet but Sonny waves it back. "No, I insist. It was great to meet you."

It was great. The whole breakfast was great.

Since I met him, I've always found Sonny easy to get along with. Here, in the informal setting of the diner, with Fitch sitting beside me, I find my mom more relaxing as well.

And I'm definitely well-fed to go into my last session of camp.

Fitch excuses himself to talk to somebody he knows at the bar. I'm pretty sure he wants to give me a few minutes alone with my mom and ... well, I guess he's my stepdad; or nearly. I'm pretty sure my mom will marry Sonny one day. I hope she does. I think he's good for her.

As soon as he's out of earshot, my mom leans forward. "Now Lacey, listen, while this has been lovely – and that Fitch is adorable –" she winks at me and my toes curl into the soft rubber of my flip-flops; *Mom approval - ewwww*, "– we did come for a reason."

*Oh no. Here we go.* I roll my shoulders back. Stretch a smile across my face.

"Sonny spoke to me after you were home the last time." She

gives Sonny a look that would be sickening in its sweetness, if I didn't also believe it was genuine. "And he made me realize I may be too close to you to be objective. You're my little girl, and you mean the world to me, but I also trust Sonny's judgment, and he tells me he thinks you're making a good decision about school. The right decision for you, anyway. So ..." She lifts her hands and shifts her weight back, "I'm going to back off."

"Oh!" Whoops, the surprise and relief in my voice are evident even to me. *Maybe tone it down a bit, Lace.* "Well, thank you."

My mom laughs. "Oh, I'm not as bad as you think I am. In fact, there's something else, but I'm going to let Sonny tell you."

"Oh-kay." I turn to Sonny.

"Lacey, if you'd decided to stay in Kingston and go to school, your mother and I were prepared to offer you a place to live. I've made an estimate of what the monthly costs would have been of having you stay with us, and I'd like to give you that amount each month that you're at school to help with your costs." As he's talking Sonny's holding out a cheque. "This is for August, because we would have wanted you to get settled before school started."

I take the slip of paper and stare at it. "But, this is too much. There's no way it would have been this much."

Sonny lifts one eyebrow. "Are you questioning my business calculations?"

Aaah ... OK, so Sonny wants to pretend this is a business transaction. Well, who am I to argue with him?

"No, of course not! If it's a business calculation I guess I have to defer to you ... and say thank you."

⟨⟨⟩⟩

In the parking lot behind the diner I hug them both before we get in the car. "Thank you both so much." I hold the cheque up. "This makes a huge difference."

As we drive back to camp, Fitch snakes his hand across the backseat and takes hold of my pinky. 'Everything OK?' he mouths.

I look at my mom and Sonny's backs, look at Fitch, and stick my thumb up in the air.

He gives my finger a quick squeeze. His mouth forms, 'Good.'

*Good.* Yes. It really, really is.

# Chapter Thirty

I never thought I could forget the island light, the softness of the breeze, the fields alive with birdsong, but I did – a bit – because once I've led Night off the trailer and I'm standing beside him, watching him lift his nose and flare his nostrils to his new home, it all seems new to me too.

At the beginning of the summer I also didn't think I'd be missing anything about camp, but for a second the hilly terrain, thick woods, surrounding the camp, and craggy Canadian Shield cradling Fitch's magic swimming hole float into my mind.

I smooth a hand down Night's neck. "Do you miss home?"

He turns his head to me and I bury my face in the waves of his forelock. "That's OK. This is your home now. You'll like it. I promise."

Salem and Jessie lift their heads from their grazing. They amble at first, then Salem trots and Jessie follows her. They push their chests up against the fence rails and prick their ears forward at this new horse in their space.

As much as I could see the hitch in Salem's stride as she trotted in our direction, I can also see the gloss of her coat brought out by the evening sun, and the brightness of her eyes. She's happy, and – if not sound – she's healthy. She's fine.

Meg comes out of the barn. "Jared's just going to park the trailer. Do you need anything from me?"

I shake my head. "I don't think so. It's still OK to put him in the paddock next to those two tonight, so they can get used to each other?"

"Absolutely. I checked the trough – it's clean and full of water. He's good to go."

Once Night is loose in his new paddock, walking the perimeter and sniffing the fencelines, Meg and I pull up a hay bale and sink onto it.

The side door of the farmhouse opens and Jared comes out, his work boots clomping on the stairs. He's got a container in his hand – one of the ancient tins his mom keeps on hand to fill up with cookies, or brownies, or whatever she's been baking.

"What is it today?" I ask.

He hands it to me, then sinks to the ground beside us. "Lemon squares."

"Mmm ..." It's all I can say as my teeth sink into the zesty lemon, sugared just enough to take the edge off.

The sun sinks steadily in the sky. The birds swoop low, and then are replaced by bats. Night and Salem and Jessie establish a game of meeting up at a corner of the fence between the two paddocks and running alongside each other to the far corner, where they turn and do it again.

"He's beautiful," Meg says.

"I hope I did the right thing," I say. "Bringing him home just as I'm leaving."

Meg bumps my shoulder. "You'll be home some weekends." My mind flips back to the corn field where we stopped briefly on our way here; Meg pointing out where Jared will mow a spot in the next field over for people to park, Jared walking one row in to show how completely the towering corn obscures any sightlines. So, yes, it looks like the corn's grown, and the maze exists, so Fitch and I have a weekend job through the fall.

Meg continues. "And I might just be able to find a bit of time to spend with him."

Jared laughs. "She'll have him schooled and ready for his first show by the time you're home from university."

Meg shakes her head. "I won't. That's work for Lacey to do. But he won't be neglected."

Jared yawns, and Meg stands and reaches her hand to him. "OK, that's it. Jared was up at the crack of dawn working on the paths in the corn maze before we drove up to get you. It's time to head in."

She looks at me. "Are you coming?"

"In a minute." I jut my chin toward the three horses now grazing, heads just a foot or so apart, on the two sides of the fence. "I'm going to watch them for a few more minutes."

As I watch Meg and Jared walk toward the farmhouse, he puts his arm around her and she rests her head on his shoulder.

There have been times when I've felt like a third wheel with them. There have been times when their very happiness pierced lonely daggers through me. That's not how I feel tonight.

My phone buzzes and I swipe the screen to life.

Fitch: Hey, Guelph girl.

Me: Hey, Laurier guy.

Fitch: What up?

Me: Just sitting here under the stars watching the man of my dreams.

Fitch: He doesn't stand a chance once I get there.

Me: Tomorrow?

Fitch: Tomorrow, Guelph girl.

**Me:** Are you ever going to stop with the nicknames?

**Fitch:** Never. Because you're something new to me every day, and you deserve to know it.

**Me:** Oh … you nearly got me there … *heart melting slightly*

**Fitch:** You ain't seen nothin' yet, tomorrow-girl (and the day after, and the day after that …)

Night has wandered to the near fence line and I walk to meet him.

I stand, very still, and he wanders his muzzle all over my shoulders and face, blowing warm, sweet-grass-smelling breath on me.

I twine my fingers through his long mane and whisper. "'Night-night, sleep tight. Tomorrow's going to be a beautiful day."

# Acknowledgements

When I started writing this series (really, not that long ago – Appaloosa Summer was published less than eighteen months ago), I had the support of a core group of people – those you might expect – my friends and family, and a few, close, writing colleagues.

Something interesting has happened as this series has moved forward, though. Because now I have a new – and strong, and loyal, and articulate – support group. Island Series readers. You have all been amazing. You have all told me how the books make you feel, why you like reading them, and you've recommended them to others. You were all very much in my mind while I worked on this book.

I also, as always, need to thank my amazing editor, **Hilary Smith**. When Hilary sent me my first editorial email and it said "Get a drink and sit down before you open this," I knew what she was really saying was "You need to re-write this book." I also knew she was right. I did re-write the book, and I'm so much happier with it. So, if you like it too, you can also thank Hilary!

Marilyn Mikkelsen Photography

# About the Author

Tudor Robins is the author of books that move – she wants to move your heart, mind, and pulse with her writing. Tudor lives in Ottawa, Ontario, and when she's not writing she loves horseback riding, downhill skiing, running, and swimming.

She's also written:
  *Objects in Mirror*
  *Appaloosa Summer* (Island Trilogy – Book One)
  *Wednesday Riders* (Island Trilogy – Book Two)
  *Fall Line* (Downhill Series – Book One)

If you'd like to be automatically notified of Tudor's new releases, please sign up at: tudorrobins.ca/newsletter-signup.

Word-of-mouth recommendations from readers like you allow Tudor to sell her books and keep writing. If you enjoyed this book, please consider leaving a review on Amazon or Goodreads. Even just a few words really help. Your support is greatly appreciated!

*Say Hi!*

Tudor loves hearing from readers. You can connect with through her website – www.tudorrobins.ca – find her on Facebook or Twitter, or email her directly: tudor@tudorrobins.ca.

# Coming Soon

If you liked this story, there will be another book in the Island series. Sign up for Tudor's newsletter – www.tudorrobins.ca/newsletter-signup – for updates.

If you want something new to read right away, why not start Tudor's Downhill Series? Book one – *Fall Line* – is available now. Book two will be released in 2016.